The Nectar of Life
(Short Stories)

Penumaka Nageswara Rao

The Nectar of Life
(Short Stories)
Author: Penumaka NageswaRao

Published by **Kasturi Vijayam**

© **Kasturi Vijayam**

ISBN(Paperback): 978-81-960562-2-3
ISBN(E-Book):   978-81-960562-8-5

SALUTATION

I am very much happy to say that most of the stories written by me were published in various telugu periodicals and a few only were rejected. Thanks to those editors and readers.

I am very much thankful to Sri DWARAKA (my uncle and also father- in –law) story and novel writer, for translating my stories from Telugu to English. My sincere thanks to Sri.Inguva Viswanath Sir for spending his valuable time to write foreword to this book.

I humbly convey my thanks to Sri Rentala Hanumath Prasad, who recognized the ability of writing in me and encouraged me like anything. No doubt it will be incomplete if I don't s

ay thanks to Smt.Kondepudi Rajeswari garu and late Dr.Paruchuri Rajaram garu for their blessings. Thanks to my arasam frieds Mr.Penugonda Lkshminarayana and Mr.Valluru Sivaprasad. My special thanks to Smt.Goteti Lalitha Sekhar and Mr.T.SR.K.Gandhi, who inspires me to write further.

I am very much thankful to Mr.Ch.Nagarjuna Sarma, who helped me a lot in preparing the book. I ncver forget the role of Mr.Emani Achuta Krishna,Mrs.Emani Poornima and Ms.V.L.Prathyusha in bringing this book to your hands. My thanks to Mr.Narendra, proprietor of M/s,Rainbow printpack, Hyderabad.

MYspecial thanks to Sri.Malladi Raghava Sarma and t my colleagues, superiors,well-wishers and to my wife and children.

MY sincere thanks to Mr and Mrs.Gopaluni Jayaraj Chandra Salutation to my patrnts.

Penumaka Nageswara Rao
Guntur.

DEDICATED

TO

BANK OF INDIA

I humbly take the privilege of dedicating this book "THE NECTAR OF LIFE'' to our esteemed Bank, which provides bread and butter to my family since my joining on 13-08-1981.

Penumaka Nageswara Rao

NO WORDS CAN EXPRESS MY GRATITUDE

PHOTOGRAPH OF SRI DWARAKA.

I KNOW, YOU DO NOT NEED THIS THANK YOU, BUT I am doing it for myself. I want to thank you for sharing your knowledge and experience with me. It has helped me immensely in all my endeavors. Thank you for recognizing the spark in me and giving the opportunity to be what I am today.

Your words inspire me to do the best of things in life. Thank you very much for that motivation. I will always cherish those precious moments spent with you.

I never forget your comments and compliments whole translating my stories. My family feels indebted to you for your kind concern and support.

Penumaka Nageswara Rao

Table of Contents

FOREWORD

It gives me immense pleasure in introducing this compilation of translations of short stories written by Sri.Penumaka Nageswara Rao who is more of a friend than an ex-colleague.

I am sure thar Sri. Rao does not need any introduction to the avid readers of Telugu Literature. Though the literaray activities of Sri. Rao span over three decade this compilation consists of 23 stories written/published over more than a quarter century (1983-2009) an appeared in various magazines/publications.

Human nature and realities of society are reflected in their true colors in these twenty three stories.If they are relevant in the earliest of the stories (1983) they are very much sto still in the latest one (2009) a quarter century later.

Family relations and inter-personal relationships are dealt with in most effective way in some of the stories in this compilation.

children are becoming insensitive to their parents? Why? The reasons are beautifully explained in "what do you say Mr.jagannadham?'' (1996)

The growing chasm between children and father and ultimately hoping to win their love back is wonderfully dealt with in "Fathers Beware'' (1998)

A defeatist view- surprisingly- is expressed about fruitlessness in attempting to change the profit/loss relationship between our near and dear in "Drop of Milk in a pot of poison'' (2001). Our personal relations have become "commercial''

"Foreign Fragrance'' (2003) is a deceptively simple story with a strong end-message.

Different interpretations of 'interest' were dealt with in an amazing way in "Rate of Interest" (2008)

"The Nectar of Life'' (2009) tells us that respect for dignity of labour should override the hiccups of life and human bondage is strengthened only with perfect equation with each other.

Contemporary issues plaguing the society find their place in some of the stories.

There is no escape from shelling out dowry either in cash or in kind as aptly described in "of the Same Feathers" (1983)

People donot know what is good for them and unite for wrong reasons – leading to their own discomfort – for example as in ''Living together''(1987)

Our first thought on going through "A Basin Each" (1988) would be – ''well well well, now we know the reason for such a low quality of structures erected at public expenditure is so low jolts you very mcuh.

Emptions swell and tumble inside you when you come across the core theme to come-into-this-world, money to live-in-this-world and money to leave-this-world but no charge for acquisition/upgradation of knowledge in the "Most Worshipful Place''(1988)

One can only surpress a smile at the way the subtle satirical message –about the perception of paraphernalia of education – passed on in "Public Opinion''(1990)

The more we adopt technology the more we move away from the niceties of civilized life. This reality is brought out in a very harsh manner in "Listen please Listen'' (2001)

A bold message – courage to seek justice is the true purpose of education – is justified in ''Against Law'' (2002)

"Hangmen'' (2005) is a scathing attack on the present-day medical profession

"Groaning Foxes'' (2009) highlights the plight of Public Transport in these perturbed times.

"Air Castle''(1997) reveals a fantasy woven around an outrageous suggestion – but worth implementation (?)

We recollect an unpleasant incidencemore easily than a pleasant experience –is revealed in "On Forgetfullness"(2003).

As all of us know, translation is more difficult than executing literary works in original – more so from an 'oriental' language to a ''western'' one. There is always the risk of the original/true intention of the author getting diluted in translation. Still Sh. "Dwaraka'' (pseudonym of Sh.Ch.Venkata Ratnam) performed a commendable task.

All in all, the fragrance from this bouquet of stories is very heady and very lastingly fresh.

I with the author all success in all his future endeavors,

Inguva Viswanath

Hyderabad

AN ODE OF MIDDLE CLASSES

Sri Penumaka Nageswara Rao is a known name in the literary field since the pleasure of his debut anthology of short stories.

All his stories are set-in middle-class ambience. The treatment of all most all his stories needs a special mention. He is a master of rhetoric. Always he had shown much mello of wisdom and mature expression in narrating stories. He ahd attempted many a number of his stories on abroad spectrum of issues. Also, he looks forword to each story with the same vigour as he did in his previous stories considered to be his best.

The concept of stories written by him is an understanding,unsaid but not unfelt. That's what matters. He gave the ever-suffering middle classes whose angst he understood verywell. It is also observed that the stories of Nageswara Rao have left behind volmes of compressed complaints that will continue to speak for the middle class.

While concluding I could not refrain from saying that Sri Penumaka Nageswara Rao is a prolific storyteller of middle classes. A feeling of complacency is present while reading his stories.

Gopaluni Jayaraj Chandra
Hyderabad.

TRANSLATOR'S NOTE

Mr. PENUMAKA NAGESWARA RAO is a contemporary prolific Telugu Short-Story writer and Novelist who has more than two hundred published short stories and three novels to his credit.

I don't think there is any Telugu Magazine worth the name, that hasn't published one or more of his short stories.

Every story is short true to the name, with only a few down-to-earth live characters, like of whom we meet in every-day life and certainly are not imaginary.

His style is pleasant, and his language is simple like the writer himself.

He has the knack of weaving stories out of day-to-day occurrences round us. He has a mind to think, an eye to observe and a skill to weave, together with a social sense.

Each story has unity and thus satisfies the dictum of "Aristotle's beauty".

Every story has a message to convey and provision for thought. These are not just pass-time hilarity. Mr. Nageswara Rao's stories are objective while Sri Munimanikyam's are subjective.

His stories are anointed with subtle humour and sly criticism that add to the glory of Telugu literature and are sure to give you a pleasant reading.

'Dwaraka'
Turupati

A BASIN EACH

Builder Kameswara Rao is busy building houses in the colony. He was moving hither and thither supervising over the workers.

Summer season.

Any amount of water is not sufficient to quench the thirst of workers.

Some are handing the bricks over to the mason. The mason is arranging them in order in the construction of the wall.

On one side people were mixing sand and cement. Some others were carrying cement bags out of the storeroom and dropping them near where the mixing was taking place. Kameswara Rao was busy supervising, instructing and entrusting.

Just then a jeep halted there. Kameswara Rao ran to the jeep with hands folded respectfully. The engineer got down the jeep in a dignified manner. He waved his finger in response to the obeisance of Kameswara Rao.

Kameswara Rao called a worker and ordered him to get two tender coconuts urgently.

The engineer walked near the place of work with Kameswara Rao walking behind him like a cat.

"How many basins of sand are you mixing with a bag of cement?" the engineer asked the worker there.

"Sixteen sir" said the worker quite unconcernedly.

"Ah! Sixteen basins per bag! what is this Mr. Kameswara Rao? Will the houses stand at least till housewarming! At this rate I won't pass a single bill of yours. All your work is improper. I don't like it. Sixteen basins of sand per a bag of cement! No No, this won't do" threatened the engineer.

Kameswara Rao smiled gently – a politician's smile.

"Sir, what you said is right. No objection from me. From tomorrow, I shall mix only the number of basins you prescribe according to the estimate. You may appoint people to supervise over my work. When you come next you can make enquiries and find out…. But sir, I have a small request to make" a vicious smile shone in the face of Kameswara Rao.

"What is that?" questioned the engineer in disgust.

"Sir, you fixed eight basins of sand per one cement bag. Over and above that number I mix one basin in the name of our ward counseller! one basin in the name of the supervisor! Only one basin in the name of our respectful junior engineer! one more in the name of our senior engineer! One basin for our commissioner! One basin for our NMR workers you have deputed to us. They stay from morning till evening with us. What more can I say sir! One more basin for you, in honour of your honest and sincere work! After distributing one basin to each, I take only one for myself sir.... Now you calculate all the number of basins and kindly tell me whose basin I can reduce. Kindly fix up the number of sand basins per bag. I shall certainly do accordingly, right from this minute" Kameswara Rao very politely asked the engineer looking straight into his eyes.

The engineer stood silent for a few seconds and then got into the jeep. Kameswara Rao was still standing politely with folded hands.

The jeep driver started the engine. Just when the jeep was about to move, the engineer said looking at Kameswara Rao.

"Do something – as you like. But see that the buildings won't collapse at least until housewarming.

******

New Jersy (USA) Telugu Kala Samithi 1988

AGAINST LAW

For the first time in life I had to step into a police station. My legs were shaking.

Summer added to my fear and I was sweating tremendously. Wiping the sweat from my brow with a kerchief, I stood behind five in the line.

I knew that there was no need to fear when you are on the right. But if you speak direct, honest and courageous before the police you are sure to land in trouble. That idea is running through my blood since I opened my eyes in to this world- I began to understand the worldly ways. The police do you more harm than help. That idea got well digested in my body – the reason may be the cinemas we see – books we read, news papers we read – and the news we listen to.

***

On Sunday evenings we friends meet in front of a friend's shop on the main road. That has become a habit with us since long.

That Sunday we gathered at the shop as usual. Some of us were sitting on the long steps beside the shop while some were sitting on their vehicles. We were discussing politics, star T.V. programmes and the newly released picture. When we were engaged thus, a person came to us and informed that the C.I. with his men was filing cases against pushcart vendors and those who sell hot eatables. He was chasing away the soda vendors at the theatre nearby. He was making much hubbub with the vehicle owners taking away their C books and driving licenses and ordering them to go to the police station.

This is very common with the newly posted officers to gain recognition by creating such commotion among the people on the streets, particularly in the evenings. Soon we saw the C.I riding on his vehicle to the police station. There was an S.I. behind him.

Within minutes after this, some police constables came to us and informed that the C.I. wanted them to bring all our vehicles to the station.

Not able to understand their behaviour we asked "What's the reason?"

"We don't know any thing. Sir, wanted us to get all your vehicles and you to the station" the constables replied nonchalantly.

"What can he do?" so thinking all of us marched to the Police Station each pushing his own vehicle. The constables walked behind us.

We locked our vehicles and parked them outside. We walked into the station. There were some more people like us standing in front of the C.I. Licences and C books were in the hands of the S.I. that was there standing very obediently.

Our lawyer friend entered the room of the C.I. We walked behind him.

"All of you should pay a fine of Rs.50/- each" the S.I. said.

"Why sir" our vehicles were not on the road".

"So you say, you won't pay the fine!" C.I. said.

"You ask the constables you have sent. Let them say where our vehicles were when they brought us here" politely said the advocate.

"What are you?" C.I.

"I am an advocate".

"Your name?"

He answered

 "Your address?"

. . . .

"Please listen to me sir" advocate.

"If you want to argue, you can do so in the court tomorrow……. If you want to pay the fine pay it" the C.I. widened his eyes.

"Why all that. Take the fine"….,

"No. I won't take it. Said the C.I. He noted down his name, address and the number of his vehicle. He was about to cancel the written receipt.

"Sorry sir…….. We are not objecting to payment of fine. Please take this" the advocate stretched his hand with a fifty rupee note.

"No, No, I won't take fine from you sir. I shall file a petty case against you. You get the court decision", the C.I said.

"Write a case against all the six and ask them to appear at the court tomorrow" he ordered the S.I. there.

The S.I. directed us all to go in to a room with a shake of his head.

He wrote down our names, addresses, vehicle numbers on a paper and took our signatures and advised us to attend the court at 8 A.M next day.

Silently we came out of the station. We were stunned at this unexpected occurrence. Our minds turned blunt.

We very helplessly puffed off cigarettes and arrived at the tea-stall.

Each one has his own comment on the tyranny and stubbornness of the police. We made unanimous comments on the rude behaviour of the police. Cutting jokes and passing satirical remarks we spent a half hour there. We decided to meet at the court tomorrow at 8 A.M. in the morning. It was late when we reached our houses.

I read in books about the tyranny, rudeness and cruelty of the police to civilians. Movies testify to that. But it has never come into my personal experience. Hatred as well as enmity filled my mind. I could not sleep well.

We were ready to pay the fine though we made no mistake, quite helplessly and timidly. We dare not question him. We were very timid. A kind of fear brewed on our own slavish life. I could only sleep during the small hours of the morning.

The sun was shining bright in the morning. I got up from my bed, completed morning ablutions within half an hour and started to the police station.

All documents pertaining to us were sent to the court which was only next to the station. A constable there asked us to sit and wait until the arrival of the judge. We friends sat under a tree smoking cigarettes.

Half hour passed. One hour passed. But nobody called us. Most of us are employees. We have to report at our offices on time. We were very anxious to leave the place.

A broker there observed our haste and came forward to help us if we pay him just ten rupees each. We found no other go. We thanked him for having come to our rescue and paid him ten rupees each.

Within a quarter of an hour we were all called before the judge. We entered the court in a line sheepishly and stood there.

"Janaki Ramaiah" was called loud.

Janaki Ramaiah stepped aside and stood.

Do you agree?" asked the judge in a dignified tone.

"Yes sir, I agree"

"Pay ten rupees as fine"

"Yes sir" Janaki Ramaiah paid ten rupees, signed on a paper and left.

"Ibrahim" – another name was announced. The list continued "Chalapathi Rao" "Purushotham"……….. All paid the fine, put signature on the paper and left one after the other. When my name was called I too did the same and was about to go out.

Just then another person was called in "Do you agree?" the judge put the question.

"What am I to agree sir?" said the man.

This was an unexpected answer. I jerked and turned back.

"Didn't you hear all this while?"

You put your vehicle on the road obstructing traffic movement. A case was filed against you. That's why you are called here. All this has been told to you earlier. Haven't they?"

"Yes, we were told sir".

"Why do you ask me again?"

"That's not what I asked sir?"

"Then what is that?"

"You asked me whether I admit that I have made a mistake. Didn't you? I don't know what I have to admit. I can't understand sir".

We were not bold enough to put such a question. I felt happy that at least some one is asking. I have decided to go late to office or apply for leave. I stayed back in the court room to listen to what passes between the judge and the man. I stood beside the wall listening. There were twenty-five more.

"Do you agree that you put your vehicle on the road obstructing the flow of traffic? Do you agree that you have committed a mistake- an unlawful act?"

"Sir you seem to have no faith in the police. You suspect their allegation. I think".

"Mister, you are using a long tongue. To put such a question to the accused is our custom and tradition. That is our duty according to law. You must remember that the police are also men like you".

"No sir, policemen are not men".

"You are crossing your limits" roared the judge.

"How is it sir? Why do you think I am abusing the police? If I say, 'you are not a man'.   It is not an abuse sir. In my view, maybe they are angels. You don't allow me to complete my sentence. How is it if you are so angry at my words?"

"Don't talk rubbish. Answer to the point.   Do you agree that you have committed an unlawful act? Do you agree that you have committed a mistake? Do you agree to pay the fine or do you want to argue?", judge.

"Sir, if you don't mistake me, I want to tell you this. I was ready to pay the fine at the police station itself, last night. My lord, but I wanted to make an appeal to you and to the C.I. Let me tell you what had happened".

"Yes, proceed," said the judge.

"I came to buy medicines for my mother at a medical shop. Putting my vehicle in front of the shop I went in to take the tablets. By the time I turned back with the tablets in hand I found the policeman standing at the vehicle. He dragged me to the police station. I wanted to explain the same to the C.I., but he got wild and refused to listen. Otherwise I should have paid the fine last night itself".

"So you are ready to pay the fine".

"How much sir?"

"Payment of fine is admission of your guilt".

We did no mistake either legally or morally. We were falsely accused....... we were ready to pay a fine of Rs.50/- each to the C.I. We were more than twenty in number. You collected only ten from each of us. The C.I. put the government to a loss of Rs.800/-. How much fine should be imposed on the officer who caused that much loss to the govt.? If things go on like this what would be the fate of the treasury. Please think, my lord" so saying he signed on a paper and calmly walked out.

That person was a milk-man. He lives at a village beside the town. He has a little landed property. He sells milk to hotels in the town. He carries milk bottles on his moped each morning and evening.

He looked uneducated; not so much well educated at least as we are.

No education is necessary to seek justice.

What is the use of education that won't give you courage to fight against injustice? Can the educated fight for justice?"

No, they are cowards in the garb of sophistication" I said to myself.

****

Andhra Jyothi Weekly 09.10.2002

AIR CASTLE

Until the other day Lakshmipathi was like any other person. He has been working at a private firm. He has a wife and two children. Lakshmipathi is not given to audacity or luxurious life. The family was leading a peaceful life.

Such a simple Lakshmipathi has suddenly become a lakhier. This was not because he dug out hidden wealth in his small house. It was not because he had won a lottery prize. It was a prize given to him for his worthy advice.

***

Suddenly the very common, simple man, Lakshmipathi became very important in the locality. He not only got lumpsum money but also wonderful recognition and respect from all around.

All newspapers published his photographs along with a brief sketch of his life. Countless interviews, honours and presentations followed.

His office management, who used to refuse a day's leave usually, has now granted a month's leave unasked in honour of the occasion.

Relatives, friends, well wishers, colleagues, people, officials, leaders – all sent him messages of greetings.

***

Government wanted to find a way out for prevention of Economic Depression and invited suggestions from people all over the country. The suggestion should be practicable and agreeable to all in the nation. The best suggestion of all will be rewarded with a cash prize of twenty five lakhs.

***

The advertisement attracted the attention of crores of people in the country. Suggestions from lakhs of people poured in.

The government appointed a committee for this purpose. They have to peruse all the suggestions and select the best one.

Instead of selecting the best one, the committee thought it best to involve the people in the process. They short listed the suggestions and finally selected ten suggestions. They published the ten in all news papers, and advertised through radio and T.V. They asked the people to vote for the best suggestion. The one that gets the majority vote will be awarded the prize of Twenty Five Lakhs.

***

Luckily Lakshmipathi's suggestion got the majority support. Almost the decision was unanimous. The government finally gave the award to Lakshmipathi. It was also ordered that no income tax should be collected from the amount.

Several people's organizations, business organizations, common people also gave prizes in cash to Lakshmipathi. All that made another ten lakhs. Altogether the amount totalled to Thirty Five Lakhs.

All these made the very common, Lakshmipathi in to a VVIP.

Lakshmipathi's suggestion is not revealed to you. That has another story.

***

Lakshmipathi is my colleague. He has been pressing me to write a story on him since long.

Some how I fancied this manipulation. I wrote the story up to this and showed it to him.

Reading this, Lakshmipathi experienced inexpressible happiness. The shine in his eyes, the smile on his lips are proclaiming his happiness. "How nice would it be if the story turns out to be real!" said Lakshmipathi innocently. I just smiled and kept quiet.

"What is that suggestion? What is that best suggestion, you suppose I made?" asked Lakshmipathi very eagerly.

"The suggestion is not yours. It's mine" I taunted.

"Really it is yours. But so far as the story is concerned it's mine. Hope you will agree" said Lakshmipathi enviously.

"Well this is my suggestion…this too is part of the story, please remember" I said.

Lakshmipati turned his eyes on me.

***

"Now, come on, listen to me. We read of scams every day in news papers. All people connected to these scams are put behind bars. They invariably seek bail. To grant a bail the courts should charge a half Crore rupees each from the culprits. The money should not be returned to them. If the government issues such an order there won't be any depression.

Then we will be able to lend money even to America. Simply this is my (your) suggestion.

***

You have built an air castle well. I know I won't get those twenty five lakhs. But I will treat you to Tiffin and coffee at the hotel spending just twenty five. Come let's go" Lakshmipathi pulled me jovially. I followed him pleasantly – feeling glad that I could weave such a story out of my imagination.

****

Andhra Prabha Weekly 14th July, 1997

CURFEW

"Hold it well, you owl" yelled Rajaiah.

Stop your vulgar voice, I held it well………..may be the pump is not working well, or you are not pumping well "you just move the rod without blowing air" said Jayamma, his wife.

"Don't pose to be very intelligent". Rajaiah put the cycle pump beside the wall.

Jayamma cleaned the push cart with a rag.

Rajaiah arranged the highly ripened banana clusters on the cart. Some bananas came out of the clusters. He piled them all on the cart.

"See these. They are near rotten. Do you mean to take them also? Said Jayamma showing the detached fruits lying beside the wall.

"I shall take and sell them. Only two hours don't know how many I can sell. I can go out again only tomorrow evening" said Rajaiah remorsefully.

Leaving a few, whose skins gave way, he put all the other fruits on the cart.

Rajaiah tied his head-band and lighted his cigar.

People began to come out upon the road slowly. Rajaiah hastened, puffing the smoke out.

"Bananas, bananas" yelled Rajaiah pushing the cart forward.

"Come quickly" Jayamma said from behind.

Rajaiah nodded his head and moved forward.

* * *

"If you feel uneasy at home, go up to Ananthaiah's beedi bunk, spend some time and come back…. If you go in to the bazaar on your scooter, some untoward may happen who knows" said Indira with fear in her voice.

"You are unnecessarily afraid. Nothing will happen. Come on brother-in-law, we shall go up to the centre and come back" showing his disgust at his wife, Bhagavanta Rao moved out with his brother-in-law.

"Once you decide you won't listen to anybody. Go if you want. But return early. Don't get beaten up by the police" cautioned Indira.

"Sister, I am here, bringing back your husband is my responsibility, don't worry. I shall tell you all the news about the curfew, after return. In the meanwhile prepare good food for us. So saying Chidambaram took out the scooter.

"Oh! I forgot. Seems scooter has no petrol. The vehicle may give trouble in the mid way. We find very long queue at the bunk. We shall go by walk, Chidambaram" said to Bhagavantha Rao.

Leaving the scooter behind, both started on foot.

The town was under curfew since four days. No schools or offices. All roads are deserted. Police are guarding at the cross roads. Curfew was relaxed for two hours today. Relaxation has already started. People are rushing on to the roads thanking God.

Though the period was only for four days – people began to feel as though it was years since they saw their friends and relatives and exchanged greetings. They were very eager to see their near and dear.

Roads looked strange though they were the same old ones. Looking at people is provoking nearness. Simple acquaintance is enough – people were greeting each other with relieved smiles.

Employees, to whom going to office is punishment, are now craving to attend offices. Children are anxious to go to schools.

People are rushing towards the beedi bunk for news papers.

"Wait, I too shall try" Chidambaram pierced himself in to the mob.

Bhagavantha Rao stood watching the rush at the bunk. Chidambaram came out with a paper in his hand after ten minutes, triumphantly.

Both went through the headlines eagerly. After five minutes Bhagavantha Rao peeped in to his watch.

Only one hour left to remain on the road ….. Did they sell the paper at usual price or did they charge more?

"Usual rate! You are very innocent brother-in-law. Usual rate is two but he is collecting four" said Chidambaram.

"Double rate!" Bhagavantha Rao opened his mouth wide.

"Even if he says five, people are ready to buy without a word. "Didn't you see the rush at the bunk?"

"Well, well. Let us have some tea" Bhagavantha Rao moved towards the bunk. Chidambaram followed.

Preventing Chidambaram, Bhagavantha Rao, stretched his arm with a two rupee note to pay for two tea.

"Two tea" he ordered.

Pouring tea in to two glasses the boy at the stall said "Four rupees".

"Single tea two rupees?" Bhagavantha Rao was astonished.

Chidambaram paid four rupees and took the two glasses in to his hand.

"You should not question such things brother-in-law" Chidambaram gulped the tea.

"Too much injustice. So much exploitation in two hours and no one to control Bhagavantha Rao was angry really.

Chidambaram put the empty glass on a stool and moved to the beedi bunk for cigarettes.

"Time we go, come early" cried Bhagavantha Rao.

Tea stall boy began washing the vessels. Beedi bunk fellow put all the unsold news papers and cinema magazines inside, and locked the bunk.

"Cigarette cost as usual or……".

"What a wonderful brother-in-law you are! "When news papers and tea are sold at double rate which fool will sell cigarettes at usual rate?" Said Chidambaram without allowing his brother-in-law to complete.

"So you bought them at double rate!"

"Yes. You can't avoid, but why are you so surprised! My dear brother-in-law, all these are quite common these days. What can be this than exploitation?" wondered Bhagavantha Rao.

Chidambaram lighted his double rate cigarette.

"Wherever you see, there is exploitation. From the rickshaw puller to the lakhier – no exception. Each one is exploiting depending on his level. No wrong if the rickshaw puller demands two rupees more when there is vrain. But when you have to go to a hospital urgently or when you want to reach the cinema hall in time, the rickshaw pullers – how much they demand is every body's experience.

Chidambaram was enjoying his smoke and kept silent. He was listening to Bhagavantha Rao, nodding his head now and then.

They came near home talking --

"Bananas, Bananas" yelling Rajaiah was pushing his cart homeward. He was hoping to get the last buyer.

Chidambaram approached him.

"At what rate are you selling bananas?"

"Six rupees!" Bhagavantha Rao was surprised. He pulled back Chidambaram.

Bhagavantha Rao came near the pushcart, I take two dozens. Tell me how much you charge" he said.: 5:

"Take at least for five a dozen".

"That fellow offered two dozens for six rupees, we refused".

"Two rupees a dozen, what do you say?"

"No such difference sir. As I am going home I offered for five. No prifit in this." Rajaiah said very politely.

"Then it is your will".

"When I started from home several poor children surrounded my cart asking for fruits. I didn't give any. Instead of giving you at half rate, better I give them free. I get at least the satisfaction of feeding the poor children" Rajaiah moved forward without a word.

"Your offer is quite unjustified brother-in-law. He told the correct rate" said Chidambaram.

"My offer is not so ignorant. See the bananas, they are almost rotten…. He can put them for sale only tomorrow evening. I don't think they last that long. They become pulp by then. That's why I said that rate hoping he would come down to any level". Laughed Bhagavantha Rao.

Chidambaram could do nothing than look at his brother-in-law in dismay. This is exploitation from our side. Who wouldn't exploit when the time comes – he ruminated.

"People like you, must understand one thing" said Bhagavantha Rao.

Chidambaram stared at his brother-in-law with a question mark in his face.

"We don't have self-restraint like the banana vendor. Otherwise, we would not have bought the newspaper and tea at double rate or the cigarettes at thrice the original price".

However, Bhagavantha Rao's words made Chidambaram thoughtful.

****

\- Andhra Bhoomi Weekly July, 1997

DROP OF MILK IN POT OF POISON

Two O'clock. Nearly mid-night. With two heavy suitcases in both hands I got down the train. Platform has a few people moving. I felt happy to find at least those many people at that hour.

Soon I got down the train a porter approached me. I enquired with him about the next train expected at the station. He said that the train I spoke about had already departed. He said that no train comes there until morning and went about his own work. I became weak and dispirited all of a sudden. I must spend three more hours on that plat-form.

In the meanwhile, a father and daughter with a little luggage reached me. They too have to go to the village as I have to. The girl too got down the same train I did. Father met her there. By his words I could know that the train I had to catch has not yet arrived there and is a expected to arrive soon. The news made me a little happy. I have to go to the number four platform and get a ticket with my entire luggage – the two heavy suitcases. I felt the task difficult. I called a passing porter to me and requested whether he would get me a ticket from here to my place. Luckily, he agreed and I gave him three ten rupee notes. He went away with the money.

The train I alighted has moved away making the familiar sound. From a distance another train with its head light seemed approaching. The porter I have given money has not yet come. I grew a little anxious – will he come at all? Will he get me the ticket? – Just suspicion arose in my mind. I did not think it wrong giving him money and requesting him to get me a ticket – I don't mind being cheated. Still I believe that he will get me the ticket. If he did really bring I can feel sure that there are still people who can be trusted and relied upon. He will certainly fortify my belief. I believe strongly that such faith on people can only make life livable and meaningful.

Although I was deeply immersed in my own thoughts. I could clearly listen to the conversation that was going on between the father and daughter. They evoked interest in me.

"Why did you perform poor in this semester than in the last one?" asked the father.

"It is only in one subject. I did well in all other subjects" she said casually than more trying to convince him.

"Even if it is one subject it counts. You have to think of the total marks".

"What you say is true. But I thought I could not write the exam. on that day. Soon I woke up I felt giddy – soon I vomited. I felt better only after a half hour lying on the bed.

Soon I saw the porter to whom I gave money coming toward me. He is the same one. I could recognize. He gave me the ticket and was about to return me the change. I prevented him. It was not because he got me the ticket but for his honesty. He has offered to return the change. I didn't take it. He went away much pleased. I felt proud of my action. My pride was not because I could get my work done easily.

He did not think "suppose I make good with the money what can he do to me?" instead of that he very honestly brought me the ticket. I felt proud of his honesty. He assured me that we can still have faith in people. I complemented him silently in my mind.

"How is mother daddy?" the girl's voice rang in my ears.

"Your mother, she is very happy observing at least half a dozen T.V. serials. But now and then she makes enquiries about your studies".

"I informed her about my marks by phone soon I got them. Why should she worry still about my education?"

"They are passing references. Nothing more than that".

"Daddy, some fifteen days back I feared that I might break my studies this year".

"Why my dear child?"

"There was some quarrel between students and lecturers. All thought of going on a strike. The principal warned that if they do some such thing, they will all be sent home mercilessly. In spite of that some insisted on going on a strike. Somehow it did not happen whatever the reason was. We girls were really terrified about this" the girl seemed to speak innocently.

It has been announced that the train we have to take is half-an-hour late.

"After half-an-hour or an hour the train is sure to come" the father said loudly. I just smiled.

"What course are you doing miss" I asked.

"Engineering uncle – second year" said she.

"Very good" I said appreciatively.

There was some commotion. Four or five porters divided into two groups are fighting. With the intervention of a gentle man everything subsided soon.

"No strike at least for the time being?" asked the father.

"Yes, it was all over. Otherwise, we would have lost this year".

"Keep aside the wastage of one year. It would cost us another lakh of rupees. You have all come here to study. You must do it with care and dedication – why all these strikes and quarrels if not for nothing" said the father a little indignant.

"The young man did no mistake father. The lecturer put him to much trouble. He swore to fail him awarding less marks".

"You don't involve in such things dear. Don't mix with such people. If you fall in their looks you too will get less marks. How is it if you don't get a rank? Be careful" he warned his daughter, of course lovingly.

I could not keep quiet.

"What miss, did you get in to the train after eating some thing or are you with an empty stomach? I asked her.

"No uncle, I did not eat anything. It was not possible".

"Don't you feel hungry, then?"

She laughed it was like the laughter of a child.

"Don't you feel that your father has not enquired you about your food?"

She sat silent with head bent.

"Right from the minute she got down you are asking her only about her marks and college. You did not say a word about her food and health" I asked him without hesitation.

In the meanwhile the train whistled at a distance announcing its arrival on the platform.

I could not hear what he said in the commotion of the train's arrival. Probably he had said something like this – "How are you interested in this more than I".

The train stopped on the platform. We got in to the train separately. The train moved.

Friends and relatives when they meet talk about shares and cards. If neighbours meet by accident, they talk about T.V. serials. Wife and husband discuss about the family budget.

Keeping all these apart, when we meet our children, instead of talking about their welfare we talk about profit and loss. We think we are moving ahead and that our star is rising high. During the journey I was engaged with similar thoughts. The train stopped. I got out of the compartment. Again, my thoughts moved.

It would have been better if I had heard what that father had said, I thought.

If a drop of poison drops into a milk pot the whole milk turns into poison. But if a drop of milk falls into a pot of poison will all the poison change into milk?

When all human relations turned into business what would be the use of my speaking about love and affection. That is all like the drop of milk into a pot full of poison.

****

- Priyadatta – Weekly 15.12.2001.

EQUALITY

Sunday. Yawning – body pains – laziness – rolling in the bed awake this way and that without getting out. No wonder if it becomes a family custom.

Sunday should be different from the other weekdays. That's my desire and decision. That's the reason why Sunday is different to me.

My wife too begins – continues and ends the day in a different manner.

On the very day she joined duty with us, the work-maid laid the condition that Sunday must be a holiday for her. That's why I like her.

On Sundays too my wife wakes up early and awakens children even if they don't have to go to school. It has become usual with me to chide my wife every Sunday. She revolts against me.

That Sunday the usual hot words were getting exchanged between us. Just at that time my friend Murali stepped into my house. Suddenly we both became silent and put on appearances pleasant. In one voice we both welcomed him very lovingly. Morning coffee was ready in the kitchen. My wife went in and reappeared with a cup of steaming coffee.

She went in and woke up the children with silent reproaches. After that ritual, she began to attend to the household work blaming the work-maid for her absence, washing the vessels of the night. She was exhausting all her anger working vigorously.

"We shall go upstairs. I have an important matter to discuss with you" said Murali in much haste. Both of us went upstairs.

"Come on Murali, unveil your important matter" I said jovially.

"This is something unusual. I am in an extremely awful situation" he said almost in tears.

"Don't worry my dear fellow. I am here to help you. Without keeping anything in suspense you open up your mind and tell me" I said.

"Voluntary retirement scheme has come as an innovation to government employees. One can opt for early retirement and take rest at home. I think you know all about this.

"Yes, yes, many employees are making vigorous calculations of the economic benefits they get due to the option. If the amount is sumptuous they opt for the V.R.S: otherwise they continue with the job. You choose the profitable way. No need to worry about this simple problem. It's not that complicated, as to worry, shedding tears. Why do you worry so much about it?" I tried to lighten the issue.

"VRS is not a problem wih me but Savithri is creating problems" wailed Murali.

"The same principle applies to her also".

"Principles apply scientifically to all equally. The problem is who of us is to apply for V.R.S. My problem is not lumpsum money" Murali said.

I could understand the problem. He wants her to opt for V.R.S. while she insists that he should. When I told him this he laughed loud. I felt his laughter untimely.

"Why that mad laugh?" I said.

"Your presumption is behind my laughter".

"You don't know the cause for my presumption. May be that is the cause" I said a little upset.

"Please elaborate the reason for your conclusion. I shall listen" assured Murali.

"To many husbands, the money earned by the wife, is more dear than the wife. To my knowledge, most of the husbands don't like their wives doing jobs. That they allow their wives do jobs is a wonder for me. Most of the husbands want their wives resign their jobs and be house wives, as she turns very arrogant after joining the job.

After getting a degree generally women aspire for jobs either for love of money or out of craze for a job. Soon after graduation, they appear for tests and interviews and finally get the job and join with great enthusiasm and celebration.

After marriage the story takes several turns. Several misunderstandings arise between wife and husband. She gets accustomed to frequent threats and warnings of her husband. Under such circumstances the job is a solace and protection to the ego of the women. Job gives courage, steadfastness and dignity to certain women who are tortured by their husbands out of jealousy and meanness of mind. In families where there is mutual understanding, women have to attend office besides attending to household work and caring for the children and husband. The money she gets on the first of every month embalms the drudgery gone through the month. In economically well off families particularly; women do jobs for love of money and to satisfy their vanity.

I explained all this to Murali. He said "Your analysis of the problem is good to some extent. But the problem between me and Savithri is totally different. You listen to the crux of my problem and advise".

"Yes, tell me" I implored.

"My proposal is that she should continue with the job and allow me to opt for V.R.S. To start with the problem seemed very small but now it has developed in to a quarrel between us". The news surprised me.

"Convincing Savithri has become a headache with me. She refuses to listen to me. I want you to convince her some how or other. I want to opt for V.R.S." said Murali.

I felt Savithri is correct. Probably she got vexed with the job and wants to retire to look after the family.

"Had there been differences between you, she would never have asked you to opt for V.R.S. you are a lucky fellow. Her idea is noble. Do her will" I advised him.

"Well, well. I came to you with a hope that you would convince her on my behalf. You have turned the table against me. I certainly did not come to you seeking certificates about my luck and her nobility. Murali was excited.

"My dear fellow, every word I said is in your interest. You both have very cordial relationship. You love each other. Had there been any malice between you she would never have opted to resign and stay at home. You hear the reason – if the husband wants to desert his wife or the wife herself wants to say good-bye to her husband, job will be essential for her. That's the reason why most women want to stick on to the job. In case both husband and wife are employees under no circumstances would she like to give up her job which provides additional security for her. That's the reason why most women want to stick on to the job. In case both husband and wife are employees under no circumstances would she like to give up her job which provides additional security for her. That's why their number is so high………."

"So you say job is an additional security for a woman over and above the husband. She can continue with the job against the wishes of her husband. You mean, job is more than man to a woman. She can be independent of man" said Murali. "So man has lost his superiority. Time has changed in favour of women".

"Yes, certainly. Days of man's superiority have gone. Man can not torture his wife any longer. Woman's suffering has come to an end" I said.

"So the superiority of woman and suffering of man started. Power changed hands. The question of superiority and inferiority still continues. No change in the relationships in fact" said Murali.

"Whether you like it or not this is the real situation. Nobody talks about the oneness of man and woman – their inseparableness. There are men who harass the woman and at the same time there are women who are cause for all sufferings of men….. Well we are getting far away from our problem. Yours is a special problem and not general. Now answer my direct question. Why do you want to opt for V.R.S leaving Savithri to continue with the job?" I said.

"It is very simple. Probably you don't know how fetching my job is. It is one that lays golden eggs. The secret money I get is many more times than the salary I get. You get salary once in a month. My job gives me money many times a day. I have made a good lot of money that way. There is every possibility that some body gets envious and makes a complaint against me or in these bad days, kite's eye of the ACB may fall on me. If so what would be my position? Until now I have managed so well that nobody's eyes grew sore about my wealth. Now this V.R.S. has come as a boon for me. Savithri, this far is clean. No danger of ACB raid. I should not wait till too late. I want to get out of the danger (job) at the earliest. Once I retire I will be a free man. I think you understand my problem. If all my secret earnings come to light, I lose all that I made good all these years. Retirement is unavoidable to every employee as mortality is, to all living creatures. If they find out every thing before retirement, I lose all retirement benefits along with all that I earned by dint of hard work. My retirement benefits come to more than ten or fifteen lakhs. I am in constant fear of losing everything. With the money I have made good and the money I get by V.R.S, I can safely start a business – at least money lending. Savithri faces no such risk. She is as pure as snow. She gets all her retirement benefits not a pie less…. I think you know the reason now. You are more intelligent than I. Please convince Savithri, and see that she agrees to my proposal". Murali very vehemently entreated.

This V.R.S. is real boon to such corrupt fellows. Murali is fully aware that he is on the wrong side of the law and in the danger zone.

"I told you the whole truth as you are my bosom friend. Please don't reveal this to anybody and land me in trouble" implored Murali who is in much fright.

"No. No, I won't do any such thing. Believe me. I shall ever remain your trusted friend.

"Glad that I have a friend like you. Come on let us have a cup of coffee together to celebrate the occasion".

Both went to a hotel and had coffee to their fill and came out. Murali paid the bill.

Before leaving Murali implored "I told you all my secret with faith in you. Please don't propagate".

"I shall deserve your confidence as a true friend. Don't worry". I assured Murali.

"Savithri has much respect for you. I hope she will listen to you…. Time for me to go to office. Don't fail to come to my house in the evening," said Murali.

"Don't you know, today is Sunday".
"I know, I know. A fellow comes to settle the account to-day. I miss him if I don't go" said Murali with a smile.

Murali drove away on his scooter.

I began thinking over all that he had said.

"I called my wife and asked her to give me a cup of hot coffee as my head is aching".

"Wait a few minutes. Decoction is not ready" she yelled from the kitchen.

Murali's problem confronted me once more. Reforms are breeding grounds for problems. At the beginning the problems can be severe too. Reforms seldom yield public good. Definitely they fetch more money to the government treasury. That is the main aim behind all reforms.

Politicians have unified politics and business. Aggrandizement has become the motto for men and women in public service.

My wife's coffee cup brought me back to myself. I drank it and took the road to Murali's house.

He suggested to go in the evening, but I thought it would be convenient now itself.

Savithri welcomed me with much civility. I made enquiries about her health. "By God's grace this far we are quite alright brother" said savithri. "Seems my husband came to you in the morning. He told me that you would be coming here".

"Yes, yes, sister. I came to you on purpose. Now tell me your opinion about it" I said.

"What can I tell you brother, whatever we speak it is very difficult for women to work both at the office and at home. Children have grown a little older. Every morning I have to prepare them for school and then go to office…. of course these problems are common these days. Now that we have the V.R.S. facility, I want to opt for it. Every month I get some pension. I want him to continue with the job allowing me to retire. He refuses to listen to me. What can I do! please tell me." Savithri said.

"Under ordinary circumstances what you say is correct. But he has certain difficulties. Suppose he loses his job what would be his position?" I said.

"Our government is not worried about people who grab crores of people's money. If such a situation arises some way out can certainly be found out. There are courts any way. Won't they come to our rescue? Please tell me" she argued.

"If he works for a few more years his salary will increase and he can get two fold increase in gratuity than he gets now. He refuses to understand me. To tell you the truth I too sail in the same boat. If his secret earnings run into lakhs, my earnings are a digit more than that. Should I not be careful about myself? Who will help if I was caught and put in jail? How shameful would it be to me! Poor man he doesn't know all this. I know what I shoud do. Kindly don't speak any more about it. If he is so much worried about himself, why shouldn't I? I have decided once for all. I should opt for V.R.S and stay at home safe".

I was wonder struck and stupefied. I could not speak a word.

These are days of equality. No question of man domination and woman subservience. Both are equal.

Both Murali and Savithri sail in the same boat.

Murali should continue with the job and dare to face the consequences. No other go.

****

Swathi July, 2001

FATHERS BEWARE

"Your son-in-law wants a scooter mother. It will also be convenient to take children to the convent. Now we are spending not less than three hundred a month on rickshaw hire" said the elder daughter to her mother.

"What do I know all that? You tell your father. Do you think I object if he agrees to give? replied mother.

"I have to admit Ravi in to convent. They are demanding donation. Please mother, tell father to give me at least sixty thousand rupees" the younger son made an appeal to his mother.

"What can I do if you all ask me? You know every thing – you ask your father – His will is all. You ask him" said mother convincingly.

"It is better to sit with the mouth shut than ask him" said daughter tauntingly.

"It is as good as asking the wall. If you can do something good you do it. Or else leave the matter there" said the son irritated.

My children who played sitting on my chest and sang songs, I taught – children who moved about in the house bickering, so lovingly – I loved them.

I am the only son to my father. I fathered two sons and two daughters. I became father some twenty-three years ago. As the first issue was a son all our relatives appreciated me and my wife.

I and my wife felt the usual happiness when a female child was born. My friends and relatives cautioned us to be careful about spending money. I felt it strange. I can't understand even now why people behave differently with male and female children.

After the birth of two more children we went in for family planning. So we stopped with four children.

Though not all, as far as I could, I must say that I could fulfill all their wants. Though I could not satisfy them completely, I could satisfy at least some of their needs, educated them and now they have all grown up. I believe that they would surely become useful citizens.

I took all care about them. But pitifully I took little care of my self. I feel that I am victim of sweet, agreeable cheating.

In youth I managed all the family affairs like a servant. Even now I am manager of the house. Then and also now I am boss in my house –

but to what use! Now I am not a member of the family. I am just a tree that blossoms currency notes. To feel great, I am just like that tree which fulfills all the desires of my family members.

My people come to me whenever they feel the need of money, they remember father. Love for father sprouts in their minds just then. Once I give them the money they want – the same old story recommences. Without money I am nothing to them.

They have nothing to discuss with me intimately. They find no time to sit with me lovingly.

They behave in such a way that they almost forget my presence in the house.

There was time when my children were afraid of me; when they don't dare to stand in front of me. In times of need they used to come to me frightfully and ask what they want very politely.

Such behaviour with my children was not their own. Their mother was responsible for all this. In her view the business of father is controlling children carefully. To be stiff with my children has become my habit. To be timid and humble became the habit of my children. This hiatus has been created between us some how.

My children showed the school progress reports first to their mother. She did not at least chide them lovingly. She would simply say "show your father – he will feel happy.

In the bed room at night she would say with me "you are not taking any care of the children. They are getting spoiled and finally turn out to be useless. The boy got less marks in Social Studies. The elder daughter fared better last time in Mathematics…….." She used to tell me about the performance of each at the school.

"Why didn't you chide them yourself?"

"Who cares for my word in the house?" she would say smiling. "They are not afraid of me, that's why I am complaining to you. If you don't warn them they won't get good marks at school. When everything is over there won't be any use of wailing…. I have told you and did my duty….. The rest is left to you" she used to caution me.

Next morning I feel pity looking at them coming to me with progress reports in their hands shaking.

I just want to take them in to my arms, and kiss them and tell them some thing endearingly. But remembering the warnings of my wife I become stiff and behave differently with them.

I used to warn each in a different way, until I feel that my wife will be satisfied with my warnings. With this kind of behaviour I made my self a very cruel task master with my children. I left my mark with them like that.

Probably such instances were the cause for my present state of affairs.

Just as they look at the clock for time - Just as they look at the fan for air – my children look at me for money - Demand and take it away.

When they wanted to go on a picnic or excursion along with the other children at the school or college – they used to go to their mother, request her, cajole her and do everything to please and melt her.

"What can I give you? If your father permits you to go, I have no objection" she would tell them.

Very soon she comes to me saying "tomorrow they want to go on a picnic. Simply don't nod your head. Still they have not come of age to go on such trips. We read horrible stories in the news papers and on the T.V. Just tell them "not possible"

"Let them go dear! They too want to enjoy life with friends" I say.

"Don't support them in every aspect. They won't care for me when they grow old. I just don't like to send them now". She puts forward some such excuse.

"Daddy, today is the last date to return our progress reports to the H.M".

She always puts the blame on their health, bad atmosphere or some such excuse for their poor performance at the exams. Listening to her, I soften and she has the upper hand.

"Daddy today is the last date for us to give names and money for participation in the picnic. Permit me to go father…." they would plead endearingly.

When they say 'Don't you allow me papa" with tears in their eyes and face filled with anxiety, 'I say "not now" with utmost difficulty. I could not dare to look in to their faces discouraged and disillusioned. The feeling of guilt depresses me.

By and by I became an enemy in the looks of my children.

After they have grown old and approached me for money, I used to refuse to give them wantonly with a fond hope that they would plead with me and sit with me trying to convince but they would go away angrily calling me stingy and miserly. Perhaps they feel that I am a brute who doesn't care to see his children happy. They have begun to neglect and look me down.

I got all my children married. All are employed. They have their own wives and children and their needs and happinesses. They have their own problems in the solution of which I am totally not needed.

They reveal their hearts sitting round their mother. They share their joys with her. I have become a spectator having nothing to do with their joy or sorrow. I feel very much neglected and lonely and began to yearn for their love and affection.

To be true it was I who taught them how to walk and how to speak and played with them. Now that they have grown up and could think for themselves and know what love is, I lost the chance of speaking to them with love. I think I have lost the essence of life. With the insistence of my wife in the name of discipline I deceived myself. I lost so much as a human being.

If they came late from school their mother would say "I shall tell your father" when they got less marks in their subjects she would say "Your father will be angry with you when they play she would say "I shall tell your father and he will beat you….." In their minds my place was that of an intimidator. I was forced to play the part of a threatening devil.

Whenever they lost their books or the newly bought pen she used to complain against them. She used to order me to punish them.

That way Madhavi, the mother, became very dear and approachable and I remained a stranger to them.

Are there not fathers who love and care for their children more than their mothers? Curious thoughts confront me from all directions.

Really I am strong money wise and am in a position to help them all in need. Suppose I give all that I have whenever they ask what about me and my necessities! The idea that they leave me helpless and the idea that they may begin to love me after emptying are at logger heads. I want to prove to them that I am not money minded and that I love them more than I love money. Fear and hope are confronting me all the time.

Can any one buy love with money? How to win their minds keeping the money with me? I am in a dilemma. I have made up my mind to share my feelings with my children and win over their unstinted love. I have decided that that can be the proper solution to my problem.

I hope that they will understand their father. If they don't, my position will get much more worse. I am prepared to face both.

My children have become parents. Now I think it is my duty at least to warn them of the travails of a father. I started my attempts.

****

-　　　Swathi Monthly, May 1998.

FRAGRANCE FOREIGN

Seshagiri is distantly related to me. His son, young Satish got a job in the U.S.

Before leaving for the USA, Satish came to me seeking my blessings and best wishes.

A month after this, I phoned up Seshagiri to know about his son's welfare.

This is what he has said –

"Satish has to travel a distance of sixty kilo meters morning and evening every day. That is the distance between his residence and work place. He covers the whole distance in just twenty minutes in his modern car. The roads there are such nice and safe".

In our country it takes two or three hours to cover the same distance, particularly in our state owned buses, provided there are no Rastha Rokos or bandhs, on the roads full of pot holes.

We imitate foreigners in dressing, dancing, growing beards, hair styling, putting on sleeveless jackets and so on. We don't take their example in laying good roads and in working hard to make honest living. Such things are taboo for us. If some one dares to say such things, it is like blowing conch before a deaf man. We imitate their drinking, dancing and easy methods of making money but never care to learn whatever is good in them – in fact our mind rebels to take such things. We waste time in gossips avoiding work. We enjoy laziness – no comparisons in this aspect.

We speak more and do little while they do more and speak little.

Listening to what Seshagiri has said – that has been my reaction.

We say roads in America are excellent and at the same time are we not aware how bad our roads are? We put up slogans every where 'Good roads are symbols of civilization. No body equals us in slogan raising. Money meant for highways safely runs in to the pockets of the selfish. Not knowing honest life we live almost dead.

After a few months Seshagiri came to my house. After going through the usual formalities Seshagiri said with a beaming face "Satish sent me a cheque for five hundred dollars".

Five hundred American dollars are equal to more than twenty thousand rupees in our currency. Ten thousand rupees on an average per month, comes to a lakh and twenty thousand a year. I made quick calculations in my mind.

Seshagiri shared his happiness with me and left after a while.

In my childhood I heard stories about card players who lost their all, including ancestral properties, in the gamble. Now the number of insolvencies due to card gamble has come down a little. This down trend is certainly not due to change of attitude but it is because several more remunerative opportunities have cropped up. The main feature of these avenues is that they won't come under gambling laws. Some of the schemes are sponsored by the government.

Playing cards with stakes is a crime even now. News papers carry news of police raids on card gambling dens and arrests.

Then, card playing was the only known social malady. Several families took to begging on streets losing their all in the gamble. That used to be the wide spread passion those days.

Now we have any number of schemes and companies luring people promising high returns for their paltry investments by installments. Offer of rebates is countless. The main idea behind every rebate and installment, is cheating. People know that they are being cheated but to no avail. Our vulnerability always tempts us to be cheated.

Making easy money is everybody's prime interest and concern. Their avarice leads them into the cheats' web. End has become all important than the means. Earning money by hook or crook has become the touch stone to measure all abilities.

As a result cheats pass for honest gentlemen and have their sway on society.

Hither to government officers were given grades – Grade I, Grade II etc,. Now terrible cheats are graded and honoured.

* * *

Latest news about Satish ---

Satish is in love with an Andhra girl in the U.S. The girl too is willing to marry Satish. As she is also employed no dowries, and other formal presentations. The girl's elder brother mediated every thing. The groom's parents were informed.

Instead of falling in love with some American girl, Satish chose an Indian girl. That too a girl of the same region, language and above all same caste. Nothing to object in the groom's choice.

Seshagiri was highly pleased with his son's choice. He sent invitations to all near and dear announcing the wedding.

Construction of houses and celebration of marriages used to be considered very problematic. Now they are no problems at all provided one has money.

No need to search for a groom or a bride. News papers and marriage bureaus provide ample information about boys and girls. They give full bio-details.

T.V. Networks put on shows, proposals for marriage from all parts of the world.

Time has changed. People's mind-sets have changed. Change is natural and can not be prevented.

The bride's parents along with her elder sister and brother-in-law came all the way from America to settle the alliance. Seshagiri was very much pleased. All joined together and fixed the convenient date, time and venue. The celebration will be luckily in India.

The bride and the groom will arrive in India just a day before the marriage. On the very fifth day, after the marriage, they have to leave for America. Being new entrants into the job, they could not get much leave. That's the reason why they can not stay longer.

Now that the date and time of marriage are fixed, arrangements for the celebration started at Seshagiri's house.

On the very day of his arrival in the town, Satish came to my house. Although his father has given me the marriage invitation, he came purposely to invite me personally. I was damn pleased with his love, respect and concern for us. US money has not changed his nature.

"How is your life in America?" I enquired.

"Very good uncle. People there are highly disciplined, punctual and they love work. I like their way of thinking, neatness, civic sense, sincerity, simplicity……".

He is in a hurry. He could not stay long. He cut short his speech and stood up to leave.

"Uncle, all of you must grace the occasion and bless us. You are my first personal invitee. We shall meet again" he said.

"Children should be like that. Satish is really very good" said my wife sitting beside me.

After making some money people pose great. Satish is very polite and humble. He is quite unlike the others. Satish is very good". I agreed with my wife.

"Only merit counts in America. Those who really deserve get jobs there…. In our country recommendations of ministers and threats of rowdy sheeters get jobs" said my elder daughter.

"People occupying high positions mix with common folk freely, there…. Here even ex-ward members and retired beaurocrates demand security to come out of their houses and behave like demi-gods. Ministers are enclosed in security rings of the police. We have another type of fellows who tie ribbons round their heads and do all sorts of mischief in the name of their favourites. That is another dirty show" I said in disgust.

After going round America and Andhra we went in for dinner.

***

Satish's marriage was celebrated with much pomp and pageantry.

The bride looked very beautiful. She was an embodiment of humility. Seemed they are made for each other.

Satish introduced me to his wife. She bent down and touched my feet in reverence. After having a sumptuous dinner we returned home.

***

Years passed by very quickly. Now Satish is father of two sons. Sashagiri has become old. He wanted to have his son with him in his last years.

Honouring his father's wish Satish returned to India bidding farewell to America to take care of his old parents.

"I am coming to satisfy their wish" he wrote to me.

I wanted to go to the airport to receive him and his family but my wife's ill health stood in the way.

***

Satish came to my house in his car with his wife and children.

We received them in great joy. Both the boys looked hale and healthy and attractive. The children speaking chaste Telugu impressed me immensely.

Before departing "Uncle here is a small gift for you" said Satish taking out a bottle from his bag and put it in my hand.

Satish's wife has already given some household utensils to my wife in the kitchen. She was explaining how to put them to use. They brought some toys also for my grand children.

The bottle Satish has given me is rather big. I could not open it. Satish took the bottle in to his hand and opened it very easily.

"You like perfumes. I brought it specially from America for you. This is something special" so saying he sprayed it on my clothes. Very nice scent. The whole room was filled with its fragrance.

He put the bottle in my hand. I was filled with emotion. I held both his shoulders and said "I feel very great about you Satish, you gave up your lucrative job in the US and came back to India to serve your parents in their old age. I congratulate you heartily". My eyes filled with tears of joy. I noticed sweet smile of fulfillment in the face of Satish who was sitting in front of me.

"Dear Satish, as an elderly person I want to tell you some thing. Please don't think otherwise". I said.

"No, No. Nothing of that sort uncle. Elders must say and youngsters should listen dutifully" said Satish.

"I venture to tell you only with such faith. This scent you have brought must have costed you much. It is really very nice. But its fragrance lasts only for a short while. The discipline and work mindedness and other noble qualities you have observed in America are the real fragrance. You should practice those qualities in your daily life here. Let our people imbibe those noble qualities. Those noble qualities are the real fragrance. The scent you have sprayed will evaporate and vanish in no time. But the fragrance of discipline and hard work will last long ……" my throat choked and I could not speak any more.

Satish held both my hands and said "certainly uncle, I promise to do my best.

The family got into the car and drove back home. We stood waving our hands expressing our happiness over their pleasant visit.

****

Jayam Weekly Jan 2003

GROANING FOXES

"THE BUS BELONGS TO ALL OF US. WE SHALL KEEP IT CLEAN".

These letters gleamed beautifully like pearls. They are very attractive. But our thoughts….. No shape – hatefully deformed. Whatever it is they are not in proper order.

"Sir, the bus belongs to us all – that far it is well and good. No objection. But keeping it clean is none of our business. Doesn't it mean that we are all bus cleaners? spoke a drunken voice.

"Well said friend. I didn't get the idea myself. Though I saw it any number of times, my bulb didn't burn until you said". Another drunkard added his voice. The words spoken by the two drunken fellows spread like wild fire all round every where and the half-awake became united. They made it a point to break the window glasses of buses into pieces". "These writings demean the youth" they raised slogans. They damaged all stationary buses. "There are people employed to clean buses and keep them tidy. It is their duty as they are paid for that. Money for them – responsibilities for us – No, no this can't continue for long". They shouted slogans highly animated.

To stop the menace, coordinating committees were formed – Advisory committees took shape. Several well meaning persons came forward for consultations and counselling. They all tightened their waists to bridge the gap between the youth and the future of the nation and to solve the problem. To stop destruction of buses temporarily, they mediated between the youth and the management of buses and came to an agreement that the writings in buses should be changed – after prolonged discussions, arguments and counter arguments from both sides.

"This is our bus – Let it be clean" is the change that has been agreed upon. Every one appreciated the decision. Government think – Tank took a breath of relief thinking that a solution is found to the problem, though temporarily, at last.

The movement subsided after hundreds of buses were damaged. Youth volatility subsided. Half burnt buses were still smoldering.

***

Respect for women is our tradition – we shall allow them to occupy their seats" – Sumathi read the words that shone right in front of her. Anger, shame and distress sprouted in her mind suddenly.

"India is a country where women are worshipped. Why should we be treated so mean as dependents on the mercy of men. – How can we tolerate this injustice –How can we keep quiet – No No No – Why should some fellow allow us to sit mercifully. Why should we crave for the sympathy and grace of the dirty men folk? What is this if not male chauvinism – A disgrace to feminity – we cannot excuse or ignore such writings. Who are they to let us sit? Don't we have our own rightful place in buses? – All these are inexcusable crimes – we no more allow such writings in buses.

They raised slogans in the name of Telugu Mahila – Jai to Telugu Mahila' placards appeared in nooks and corners of the state, villages not excluded.

This incident united the women folk everywhere. We won't stop this agitation until writings on bus seats are removed". They hurled their anger in the shape of stones whenever they saw a bus. "The very sight of the bus was hateful to them. They hissed like cobras at the very appearance of buses.

Wearing silk saries, ladies went on processions in towns holding placards in hands. No wonder their gold bangles sparkled bright in the sun. They shouted slogans through loud speakers. They appealed to the public for support, enlightening them how they are ill treated in buses and sought their unstinted support for their cause claiming to be just. They demanded a change in the writing on seats. "Respect for women is our tradition – we shall sit only after they take seats". Some how this agitation also subsided.

***

"Close down all Telugu Medium schools" "Telugu Medium schools must be abolished forth with".

"Must be abolished – must be abolished" slogans.

"Telugu Medium schools must be abolished immediately".

A big procession, consisting mainly middle-aged people thronged the streets. They were shouting slogans. There was anger and passion in their voices and beat in their steps. There were some school going children in their midst here and there.

"Telugu has no future – we don't want it".

"We don't want".

"We don't want".

"We love and like English Medium".

"We love and we like".

"What about is this agitation? Who are they"? Questioned a passerby.

"They are parents – parents of convent going children".

"So their demand is that they don't want Telugu medium schools".

"What do they propose to do?"

"What do they do – From tomorrow they hold up traffic on roads – they won't allow trains to move. They break buses and if it comes to that they burn them".

"A good thing" the passerby went by laughing. The English medium schoolteachers and managements joined the agitation on the next day in support. They want the removal of Telugu as subject of study from syllabus. They want the reduction of school bag weight.

Krishna Devaraya, the mighty ruler patronized Telugu proclaiming that no other language is equal to Telugu. He was a great Telugu poet himself. These people are fighting for the removal of such Telugu from schools" wailed some people of old times. The hi-tech propagandists shut their mouths with clever arguments.

They proclaimed very loud that they won't allow the schools to open until and unless their demand is met. Some organizations too extended their sympathy to the agitators. No wonder that some politicians and their parties extended their wholehearted support to the agitators who are ever ready to cash on such exigencies peacefully!

Schools did not open their doors. There was bandh. So parents and children did not move out of their houses.

One Day –

Mediators intervened. They called both sides for talks. After drinks and other beverages, they held patient discussions and at last arrived at an amicable solution.

The crux of their decisions is –

1. The number of Telugu medium schools will be limited and will be allowed only to the extent necessary. For the present, they close down the Telugu medium schools in gradual stages and finally recommend their

abolition altogether.   Until then without taking the medium into consideration, whoever writes Telugu paper at the examinations will be awarded cent percent marks in the subject – and these marks also will be taken into account while deciding ranks. As a win-win agreement Telugu teachers can continue in their jobs and the agitators will have their demands accepted. The agitators were satisfied, and the situation has not grown serious to the extent of burning buses somehow.

***

"Censor board down – down".

"Suspend immediately the members of censor board".

Shouts, cries, slogans of youth with red – ribbon-head-bands – dances, drumbeats, acrobatics, songs and what not. They stood opposite a bus that came that way.   The driver stopped the bus. They ordered all the passengers to get down. They divided themselves into groups. One group was busy removing air from tyres. One group got into the empty bus and vacated the remaining passengers; kicked the seats and cut them with blades into pieces.

"Why all this young man? Why are you damaging the bus?" ventured a sixty-year-old passenger to ask daring the consequences.

"Do you want to know why? The film boxes have not come yet. We have come to know that the cause for the delay is a censor board member. That's why we took to agitation" announced one from the group proudly.

In a certain town, the favorites' association of a certain film star went on a rampage because the cinema of their favorite hero was not released on the announced day.   The Favorites' associations all over the state got the news of the late release of the picture and as a result all favourites'associations of the hero organized Rasta Rokos… bus burnings and other destructive acts. They took to the same type of agitation; all association members invaded the censor board office. Countless number of buses were damaged. "We don't mind whether the picture is obscene or otherwise. We want the release of the picture here and now. It must be screened immediately at any cost". Pleaded the important social workers. They suppressed the volatility of the youth and prevented the loss of more buses.

***

High ranking government officials at last opened their eyes and collected the loss estimates at various places. After several additions and subtractions, multiplications and divisions, they arrived at the total loss caused and also have taken into account the recent increases in petrol and diesel costs and finally decided to increase the bus ticket fares.

Another agitation erupted to safeguard the interests of commuters. Some more buses were destroyed. A compromise meeting was held between the government and the agitators. A little of the proposed price rise was reduced. All parties agreed to this arrangement. Remaining buses came on to the roads fearing further attacks.

***

Soon an important political leader died …. no, no was killed – not clear yet whether he died on his own or was killed. Whatever it is, a bolt from the blue fell on the heads of RTC buses. It was like a curse on the RTC buses. The dead leader was born, bread and died amidst faction rivalries. These factionists kill rivals and get killed. The death of such a leader created another storm in the state. Angry crowds burnt down hundreds of buses, Brutes had their field day.

***

Whatever the reason was, public properties were burnt down to ashes.

Already the poor taxpayers are moaning under the weight of taxes – taxes and more taxes. If further taxes are hurled on their heads – they are sure to die, who can save the multitudes of unfortunate destitutes?

Why won't they raise their voices against all the attrocities? They just groan silently getting crushed. – The groaning foxes! They just groan and never rise up. Why won't they at least shout!

-        Navya Jan.21, 2009

****

HANG MEN

I

Age Sixty-five, weight sixty seven kg., Height over six feet, complexion neither fair nor dark.

Body limbs not under complete control. Mind wailing hard. Life blinking. Wants to disclose something. Grief stricken – not able to speak out. Afraid of silent death. His misery, he could understand. Memories innumerable. Desires fulfilled – unfulfilled ambitions he could never realise – Times unfavorable – inextinguishable anger – world weary – dislike – disgust. Drooping eyes – burning body – skinny legs unable to bear the weight of the body – pain all over – fingers twisting with numbness – recognition getting lost – degenerating health becoming critical – pain – sorrow – changes brought in by age and habits - All put together on the threshold of the end – satisfaction that he had done something to his near and dear according to his ability – life has given him much – learnt much – repaid much – How much remains in the end he can't decide. He is not able to calculate all. Crowding his mind, philosophical thoughts.

***

II

Her man for over four decades is in bed suffering hell. She could not bear the sight of him. The person, who has been a pillar of support for her, is now in bed seeking help. His condition is miserable. She must pick up courage – She must save her god – like husband.

She too is suffering – moving in and out – he, in bed motionless.

She took up courage. Made a determination, stood up. Phoned up for the ambulance and dialed two or three numbers and told them the news.

In another fifteen minutes the ambulance stood in front of her house. She opened the almirah – collected all the money inside. Put it in her pouch. A young couple came to help her. All helped to put the patient inside the ambulance. Locked the door – she sat in the ambulance beside her husband. The van moved. The couple moved behind the van on their vehicle. The journey was to the hospital with mountains of hope – hope that they would save her dear husband.

Over forty years of association, one lived for the other. Any number of shared experiences – anger – threats – abuses – love –happiness- experiences all that life contains. Relatives came to them showering affection – praise – appreciation, all to have their selfish ends served. In their pitiable condition no one showed his face. They were victims of scandals for no reason. All these, part and parcel of life drama. Memories of the past rose up like stinging wasps. The ambulance reached the hospital in the meantime.

***

III

Dirty odour – pungent smell of spirit, medicines, patients and dirt. Environment hideous- welcomed them.

Van stopped at the hospital gate. She got down. The young couple helped in putting the patient on the hospital stretcher.

The patient brought to the hospital, was kept in waiting.

***

IV

The doctor was in his chamber. Patients suffering from all sorts of diseases were waiting.

The swing door of the doctor's chamber was busy swinging. A young man in uniform was busy ushering patients in and out. Nurses are busy moving with writing pads in their hands. There was dignity and style in their walk signifying importance.

Our patient's chance came at long last to be pushed inside the doctor's chamber.

The doctor did not move from his seat. On seeing the patient the doctor asked "What's your name?". The patient was groaning. The wife answered.

"Where do you come from?"

She replied.

"What is his problem?"

She speaks

"Why did you keep him so long without bringing him to the hospital?"

She explained her difficulties.

The doctor did not move from his seat. He did not test the pulse nor use his stethoscope. He did not speak any hopeful words.

"You kept him in your house without treatment this long and brought him to the hospital in the end. If something happens, you blame us", the doctor said in disgust.

Although he could not speak, the patient could hear the words. They were quite disheartening. They could turn the well wishers of the patient in to patients.

***

V

The old habits of testing the pulse of the patient and examining the tongue etc,. have vanished from the profession long back. They have become out dated practices. Old methods have given way to the new ones. Several instruments have stepped into the profession.

Doctors today breathe fear and despondency into patients. They don't say a word that sooths the patient.

When you go to the person, called 'doctor', his soothing words must cure half his disease and fill him with hope of recovery. That's why a doctor is compared to God and praised as life giver.

The whole trend changed with the present day doctors. They speak harsh and prescribe umpteen tests. Suppose somebody asks "why all these tests?" They have the ready- made answer. "We must be careful about ourselves first. Tomorrow if something untoward happens who will come to our rescue?

"Government and people guillotine us mercilessly. These tests are our saviors. First we must know the cause of the disease. Then only can we prescribe the cure. Without knowing the cause how can we cure?" This is the argument of the saviors of life.

***

VI

Doctors too are human and have their own problems. We must find solutions to those problems. We can not punish the whole profession for the wrongs of a few.

They spend lakhs of rupees to get a degree in medicine. They have to spend many more lakhs in the construction of buildings and purchase of necessary equipment. They have to spend on nurses, ward boys and others. They have to meet all these expenses without fail. Without money they can not put up any show. Patients are attracted more by show than by proficiency. They must find means to get money. They took up the job certainly not to go round courts and answer enquiries.

"We don't like to make life a problem for us. We too want to live…. we can try to prevent death – but can't breathe life into patient. When the patient recovers people say we are gods. Suppose the patient dies they throw heaps of abuse on us and call us harbingers of death and call us murderers. People have forgotten ethics….. By the by, are all lawyers fighting for justice? Are those who call themselves engineers caring for quality in their work? Do they take proper care while laying foundations of various constructions? Several buildings fall down at the time of construction, like a pack of cards. Several innocent people die under the debris. Who is responsible for all those deaths? Are we not better than those people? We don't kill but try to save and in the end leave them to their fate and to the mercy of God".

***

VII

Thoughts lurking in the mind of the patient –

You have your own arguments and problems. First think of me. Change me to a bed. I am very uncomfortable on this sheet of iron. Then you can think of medication.

"When I feel a little comfortable – you can think of medicines".

They charge six hundred a day for allowing the use of bed. That is a mental torture. Silent suffering without telling any body.

Some body came and administered two injections. "Oh, pierce, pierce needles. I am at your mercy. The body is entrusted to your care. What else can I do? Can't escape punishment for the past deeds. I don't object. But doctor, a word with you".

"We are those of the fellows who can not make both ends meet. Ours are decrepit lives. So don't try to scratch away our lives like jackals. Seems in some town you built your dispensaries in a line. It is said that the street has become well known as 'jackal lane'. The name is very apt I think. Let every street in which you built your hospitals be called 'Jackal

Street' in common – so that all patients know it well without mistake. That is my wish.

"Just because body temperature increased, somebody comes to you for help out of fear. You ask him to undergo all sorts of necessary and unnecessary tests. You keep him in bed for a week and collect twenty or thirty thousand rupees to say finally that "you have no disease" and send him away. What sort of doctors you are! How can you be called doctors? Please introspect at least once".

"Seats are allotted for those who got three hundred marks as well as three marks in medical colleges. Without reference to merit, degrees are given to one and all. They all transform themselves into doctors and play with the lives of innocent people hanging the stethoscope in necks".

"Government hospitals. Many have become free choultries not meant for patients. The so called doctors won't have any control over the other employees in the hospital. Some times ministers, high officials visit the hospital as though on picnic. They warn every body there of dire consequences to exhibit their authority and power. Next day's news papers publish stories of the visit of the higher ups. All this has become a farce".

"Don't know how many tests you want me to undergo. My wife is quite innocent and not worldly wise. Why should she suffer on account of me?. I am able to listen to all you say. Doctors are called life givers. Please be merciful. Don't be butchers. No objection to your making money but let it not be by cheating. Don't perform unnecessary operations. Don't prescribe unnecessary tests. Don't speak harsh and frighten your patients – please give them life not death. Patients die but doctors live long. You doctors listen to my silent words".

"A hangman kills people. It is his profession. A certain hang-man, I read in newspapers, refused to hang a person because his mind objected to the inhuman act. He poured out his mind to the higher ups. He was ready to lose his job".

"You are life givers. That hang man is better than thousands of your profession".

"The hangman takes away life only. You take away the life of the patient and lives of all the people dependent on him by squeezing all his money. You are responsible for the death of so many".

"The hang man was more humane than you are. Take the hang-man as an example.

You count the number of people you have spoiled".

***

His eyes shut. His breathing stopped. The doctor stood watching silently.

****

Swathi Weekly 03.06.2005.

HOW WOULD IT BE!

Sunday morning. The old lady sat anxiously waiting for the clock to strike nine-thirty.

The lady got up earlier than usual-completed her bath-worship of God and the other daily chores. She spread her wet sari to dry on the terrace of her house. All this is her preparation to sit before the T.V. watching Ramayana to which she has been addicted to, since the last six Sundays. She has reverence and anxiety concerning Ramayana on the T.V.

She sat looking at all the advertisements relayed on the T.V. after 9.30 though in disgust. Just when the Ramayana was about to start, the power supply went-off. All her enthusiasm was dashed to the ground.

Think how terribly she must have suffered mentally upset and disappointed.

She cursed the electricity department and the people working in it, to her heart's content.

They don't think of cutting power when all sorts of obscene pictures are put on show. Poor fellows, they too have their own interest in such shows and they don't like to hurt their own interests and won't cut power. God damn these fellows.

Who wants these days to watch Ramayana or Mahabharata, except the old and pious people like us? When we eagerly await the show, this is what happens. Scolding all those responsible for this, she walked back in to the kitchen.

****

The power supply went-off long back in the morning. The supply is not restored yet. Camps and office work eat away all the week days. Only Sunday is left for us to stay at home and enjoy leisure but this happens with the current supply spoiling every thing. A very good cinema, Aish starrer will be on show and no power to-day. They apply power cut on Sundays alone as if they don't have any other day in the week.

News-papers proclaim that there won't be any power-cut henceforth. But the situation continues to be the same. Sunday holds no pleasure for us poor folk, working in offices.

Such are the feelings of a government employee who plans to spend his holiday happily at home.

*   *   *

"Limited Overs Cricket match between India and Pakistan to-day. My friends and I are eagerly waiting to watch the match – No power supply to switch on the T.V.

They keep the street-lights burning all day. By the time it is night they cut-off the power supply. Fans don't work in the night. People have to suffer suffocation all the night. What else can the department and the government do than put the common people to suffering?

A cricket fan's lament.

***

People are irritated and agitated, all over the town.

***

Nearly a hundred people are at work repairing a big transformer that struck work, bearing the severe heat of the summer sun.

***

How would they all feel in case they happen to listen to all these harsh blames, abuses and curses!

****

LET US BE HUMANS

The very sight of the bus strikes panic among people waiting for the bus at the bus-station for long. They won't wait until the bus stops at the specified place. They run-They shout-They pull - They push - They trample - They cry - They wail-They are men-They are women-They are children- They are adults. Some are weak - others are strong. They flock the bus on all sides. Each one looks as if eagerly rushing to grab his life's accomplishment. The whole scene resembles a civilian-war. The driver plays his acrobatics - slows down the vehicle applies brakes suddenly releases them and moves forward. The weak and the old fall down. The young and the strong run trampling their bodies.

They rush to the bus-door. They don't heed the shouts of the conductor. They don't allow the door to open nor do they allow those who completed the journey to get down.

Some throw their towels and hand kerchiefs on the seats to claim ownership later. Some get in with utmost valour and occupy seats triumphantly. The most successful are those who could occupy the window-side seats.

Even before the bus is empty, double or even triple of its capacity, fill it - people on seats, people between the rows holding whatever comes to grip.

Some pull their loved children and babies through the gaps in the windows!

I got a telegram informing that a close friend of mine had met with an accident. Luckily he was wounded and hospitalized. I made up my mind to go and see him as early as possible. I came to the bus stand. This is the situation here.

I could not brave myself to be one in the crowd and fight to secure a seat.

I stood on the platform wondering how the poor conductor could make his way from the front to the back and issue tickets!

I preferred to wait for the next bus. In another five minutes the over crowded bus left the place giving a sigh of relief.

A half-hour passed. Another bus appeared. The same scene is re-enacted. This too has gone without me. After a half-hour's interval another bus came on to the plat-form. There is rush at this also but with a little less intensity.

Somehow I managed to get into the bus and could secure a seat to my great delight.

Now that I could sit in the bus comfortably, I began to think of my friend - how he is - in what condition - how his mother and wife are - whether they have enough money for medicines and other expenses! I am very much grieved. I know I can't be of much help to my friend and his family but surely I am not so mentally bankrupt that I can't at least wish well for them. I shut my eyes and leaned back ruminating.

Suddenly I heard a burst of harsh words exchanged between two passengers. I turned my head back to have the video of the affair also.

"I threw my towel on the seat. Didn't you see?" angrily shouted a man in dhoti and full sleeve shirt in white.

"I saw no towel here when I sat. Probably you put it elsewhere. Go and search" stubbornly said the seat occupant who is in a T shirt and a checked pant under, looked like a college student.

"So my towel moved on its own to another seat at your august sight" barked the man in dhoti.

She student like youngster, sat unconcernedly as though he didn't hear anything.

"Not enough if you put on airs of a student in shirt and pant one must have commonsense" shouted the dhoti-wallah. "Shameless bastards".

"If you talk like that I shall tear your tongue into pieces. What do you take me for?" the student blew fire out of his mouth and got up.

One swears to kick while the other swears to stab. They were ready to grapple each other.

Four or five men in the adjacent seats intervened and pulled them apart. Peace apparent was restored.

The driver and conductor took charge of the bus and at last it moved.

For ten more minutes, the two warriors sat, each complaining against the other to his neighbour.

The bus stopped when it reached town out-skirts. The conductor completed the issue of tickets in another twenty minutes and shouted "Right".

The driver became alert and started the engine. The bus moved at last with a jerk.

"See sir, our people have become so foolishly selfish that they are ready to kill or die just for a seat in the bus. See the people and their passions,' said the gentleman, next to me in the seat, in a low voice as if revealing a secret.

I just shook my head without speaking.

Showing my disinterest in the matter, I opened the weekly magazine that I carried in my hand.

My neighbour fell silent and started peeping into the pages surely for a glimpse of the beauties of the tinsel world.

After a while, I shut the book and also my eyes and leaned back. My neighbour made good of the magazine and put it to his use.

Suddenly the bus stopped making a creaking sound. I got up from the nap, and opened my eyes to see long lines of vehicles in the front and several coming to a halt behind. Scooterists were rushing at great speed mending their way acrobatically, like Sahadeva of the great epic.

Endless hooting of horns in the front and from the back demanding clearance of way for further movement.

Passengers in our bus began to get down, curious to know the reason for the jam. I too got down to straighten my body and to get rid of the numbness of my feet.

The reason for the stoppage of traffic on the road reached me after a good amount of time on the road.

People of a village beside the road have been thirsting without water for the last three days. The water tanker that usually brought water to the village stopped water supply for reasons not known. The tanker with water arrived at the village at long last. The villagers rushed to the tanker for water with all sorts of vessels in their hands.

There was a struggle among them to gain advantage over the others. At the bus stand struggle was for a seat. Here struggle for getting a pot of water. None has patience to wait for his or her chance. Every one wants to undo or out do the others.

Shouts and swears are taking place at such high decibels that we at this distance are able to hear.

Latest news is that a valiant woman broke the head of another woman with her brass-vessal. The hurt woman caught hold of that woman's throat and almost strangled her to death. That was the cause for all the shouts, cries and wailings.

The villagers took sides and began to fight with sticks and sickles. Bleeding injuries to many on either side. The fight gained political tinge also soon.

A contingent of police rushed to the spot and controlled the situation without much further damage.

The woman that strangled the other, fell down as if in a swoon.

Some said she was acting - others said that the act was real.

With the arrival of the police on the scene calm after the storm was restored. Police threats - warnings - counselling - all took place.

The woman with broken head and the other that swooned were sent to the hospital immediately. The others wounded in the fight also were sorted out and sent for treatment.

Water in the tanker drenched the road all over.

Traffic moved at snail's pace as though nothing untoward had happened. Vehicles moved. Life moved as usual.

It was late in the night when I reached my destination. Two hours journey took five hours. Glad that I could reach at all! I got down the bus and engaged an auto to take me to the hospital.

I arrived at the hospital gate. The gate was closed. A little altercation ensued between me and the auto-driver over the fare - I yielded and the fellow went away triumphantly.

The gate-man yielded to a tip, opened the gate and allowed me in.

I very hastily trod in to the main building. Luckily I found two of my friends who came to the hospital as I did, earlier. They took me to the ward where my friend was. They saved me the trouble of making enquiries.

His mother and wife were sitting at my friend's bed side. The usual enquiries followed. My wounded friend was sleeping. Now-and-then he was groaning aloud.

A little composed, I looked round the ward. It is a big hall with twenty five beds. Every bed has a patient and every patient has his attendants.

I sent my friend's mother and wife to have food and rest. I offered to attend on the patient the remainder of the night. They left though unwillingly putting faith in me. All in the family know me well.

Doctors and nurses are visiting the patients in their charge, talking among themselves.

I went near a doctor and very humbly enquired about my friend's health.

He is a doctor with a kind disposition. He showed no irritation. "We are treating him. He is out of danger but needs treatment at least for a week" he said.

I decided to stay with my friend for two more days to see him recover a little more.

I pulled a stool to his bed-side and sat on it. As I sat looking into his face several memories hovered round my mind-the experiences we had together- the work we did in union- the discussions we had between us - the differences that arose - the good qualities he had and several such other things .... As memories came to my mind one by one my eyes wetted. Consoling myself - gathering courage - I sat.

All patients in the hall are victims of accidents. Probably this ward has been meant specially for them. Every patient has attendants to look after.

The fans are whirling at high speed making much sound. No dearth of air in the hall."

Some attendants are helping their near and dear while the others are talking with the others in low tones. Anxiety and concern are writ large on every face. Each has his or her own troubles. Poor fellows I pitied.

Suddenly a woman, an embodiment of grief, came to me. "Sir, please, do you have any slices of bread with you? I sent our fellow to fetch one but he hasn't returned yet. My hungry son is weeping asking for bread. I shall return soon our fellow gets" she pleaded in much humility.

Her humility moved my heart. "What a person you are, sister! Feeding a hungry child is every body's duty. You need not return. I have some milk also, if you want" I said very cordially. Moving from the bed-side, I picked up the bread that was there and gave it to her.

She thanked my good nature and went to her child happily saying that she would come for milk if the boy asks.

"How long can you stand like that? Come; sit with me on the stool. I shall make place for you", said one man to the other standing nearby. The man standing, is near bed number four.

"The stool is small. It can't hold two. You sit comfortably. I shall sit on the floor for a while", said the man to whom invitation to sit was offered.

I sat wondering about the very nice behaviour of people towards the others.

Just then a trainee doctor came to my friend's bed and said to me "give me the saline bottle. I shall arrange it and go".

I searched for a saline bottle near the bed. I could find only empty bottles. There was no new one. "Sir please no bottle is available here. I shall go and get a new one" I said.

"No, No, how can you be so careless. I shall go now" said the trainee doctor.

A young man observed my predicament. He wanted to save me out of the situation. "I have a full bottle with me. Please take this and attend to the work" he ran to the bed with the saline bottle. The trainee doctor took it and arranged it properly gave some instructions to the nurse with a pad in her hand and departed.

I looked into the face of the young man with eyes full of gratitude and appreciation. I expressed the same in words holding his hand.

"What's there in this sir? I just helped one in need because I have one with me. This morning I brought five bottles for my father - three are used and two are left with me. I gave you one."

Over powered with emotion, I shook his hand - thank you for your timely help ---- I shall return the bottle in the morning. Though you don't know who I am, you came to my rescue. Thank you, Thank you so much" I said still holding his hand.

"You need not thank me so much sir. I did nothing special" said the young man most endearingly.

Within two or three hours, all attendants in the hall became my acquaintances - men and women, young and old. Every one has his or her tale to convey. They narrated when and where the accident took place - How it happened - The injuries caused and in which state the patient is - Their difficulties with money - the services of nurses and doctors with commitment - And all.

'Suffering shared in common binds people with hoofs of steel' said the great Shakespeare. In fact the bond here is not made of steel but of love, which to my knowledge and thinking is a sense of 'sacrifice'.

Most of us spent the night awake talking, while a few slept, leaving the patients to our care most trustfully.

Most of the roads in our country are narrow, very old and full of pot-holes. Roads remaining the same old, vehicular traffic increased two hundred fold. That's the cause for many of the accidents, speedy and drunken driving are the main causes for accidents. How can we leave politics and politicians without giving importance in our discussion? There is no life activity that hasn't been polluted by them after independence.

The next day being Sunday I remained at the hospital attending on my friend and giving courage to the much grieved mother and wife. I gave them time to rest at home.

Some people in the hospital ward came closer to me like friends. Some took my address and gave me theirs so that we can keep in touch later.

The next day is Monday and I must report for duty at my office.

In the meanwhile my friend's condition has improved. In good faith I can leave on Monday morning.

Some other friends of my friend came to the hospital to wish him well and give courage.

Sunday night four of us in all ate at a hotel happily discussing the loving qualities of our friend in bed. His mother and wife also are a little happy that he will soon be out of hospital in good health.

Monday morning - Leave taking from all the new friends has been heart rending. Two of them even accompanied me to the bus-stand. While coming out of the ward I went to every patient and wished them very speedy recovery.

As I sat in the bus several thoughts began to sting my mind.

People are good by nature. But those good and humane qualities make their appearance at times of sorrow, generally. They behave very selfish when they are strong and well. How pleasant the world would be if people are tolerant to the needs of the others in all walks of life and on all occasions!

****

LISTEN PLEASE LISTEN

It is nearly a decade and two years since I married Poornima. During all these twelve years we were never alone, one without the other. Wherever we went, we went together. Stayed together and returned together. Our daughter was born three years after our marriage. Until the baby is two years, we never moved out of the house.

Such has been our circumstance all along. But now Poornima and the baby have left me alone here and went to my brother-in-law's place. I am alone in the house. Instead of claiming that I don't know cooking, it is more true to say that I prefer having food and Tiffin at a hotel rather than cook. If I spend two days that way, Poornima will return and I can be myself again.

Daily activities are going on as usual. As has been my wont - I work at the office until six in the evening and then return home. Half-an-hour reading weeklies - Another half-hour with the T.V. programmes are spent. Then I have my bath and go along the bazaar. Greetings and enquiries are exchanged with acquaintances on the road. Reach the hotel - have food - and return home at about nine in the night. Lie down on the cot watching T.V. programmes - switch off the T.V. and go to sleep. Four days passed by as if in four hours. Poornima is expected today - I gave the keys of the house to our neighbour and went to the office as usual.

****

Poornima phoned up to me, informing of her arrival at home. The journey was comfortable; the baby is quite alright and has gone out to play with the neighbourhood children. She asked me to get vegetables while coming home. Latest news about Poornima and the baby!.

After a separation of four days, my wife and daughter have come back to me. I found no anxiety to run and meet them to know the news about relatives. As is generally written in stories, I have felt no eagerness to fly and fall before them. But it does not mean that I have grown disinterested about them and is not concerned at all about them.

As usual I left the office at six in the evening - bought vegetables - and a train toy that operates on battery for the baby. I arrived on my scooter at home. Baby heard my scooter sound and ran out of our neighbour's house to see me with a pleasant face. Poornima followed her from the back with a smile on her face. I gave the toy to the child, lifted her in to my arms and kissed. Poornima took the vegetable bag from my hand.

"Seems the train has arrived at the right time" I said as if to break the silence.

It has come correctly at four-thirty" Poornima said handing me the coffee cup, she sat beside me with another cup in her hand. Baby is immersed in her play with the train.

Poornima walked into the kitchen and I took the weekly into my hand as usual.

No caption in the weekly interested me. Some sort of emptiness filled my mind. A feeling of something having been lost. Some inexplicable mental emptiness, I began to experience.

I closed the book and walked to the terrace of the house. The sky is very clear - Stars are sprouting here and there. I lit a cigarette and began to walk to and from.

My daughter and wife were not with me for four days. Remaining aloof from them so long is some thing I never had experienced.

When they returned why this unconcernedness? Every thing seems very usual and casual to me. I feel as though they are in the house all these days with me. There is no freshness in their arrival. This lack of freshness is something that I am unable to understand. Nothing new at all. Why? Is it due to lack of love for them? or is a sort of detachment taking place in me? Or is something missing from me?

Amongst several kinds of thoughts an idea flashed in my mind. "Yes, that's true" I thought. My eyes caught sight of the telephone that was there in the room without motion or word.

Yes. Soon they stepped in to the house of my brother-in-law; baby phoned up to me and spoke all about her travel experiences, without leaving one..!

After one hour again Poornima spoke to me for over half-an-hour. Later on, she phoned up to me half-a-dozen times both when I was at home or at office, every day. The phone consumed that which ought to have taken place between us, live. The lifeless phone ate away the freshness of life. How pleasant would it have been listening to her narrating all her experiences good and bad in gusto, lying in my lap very lovingly and I cutting jokes in between teasing her, munching groundnut peas or some thing!.

The lifeless telephone usurped from us all that lovely and lively experience. It left us with no news to be conveyed either by her or by me, afresh.

Four or five days after this incident, my friend Jayachandra wrote to me a letter after a long gap. I was busy with office work. Looking at the from address on the envelope, I put aside all work, tore open the letter and read its contents. He spoke about several things in his letter, but I grew very unpleasant with it.

This unpleasantness was not without reason.

We were very good friends right from our high-school days. His hand-writing used to be very beautiful. The letters looked like pearls. Students and teachers as well used to shower appreciation on his hand-writing. Every one used to admire, with girls no exception. No wonder that all got their names written on their text and note book wrappers. A few of us even got our notes written by him. Invariably he was getting marks for his good hand-writing at the examinations.

Such a Jayachandra, writing the letter so shabbily, surprised me a lot. I read the letter from the beginning to the end - memories of child hood - money problems - education of children his wife's ill health expected promotions threatening privatization inescapable transfers were discussed in his rather long letter. Lest I should forget to write a reply, I began writing immediately.

To start with, I wrote how greatly I was surprised with his shabby hand-writing. It filled a half page. Next came my personal issues, world situation, politics, conditions laid down by our work maid, advices not to join any money schemes - and all that. I folded the letter and posted it. Then I re-commenced my office work.

In the end of the letter I completely forgot to request Jayachandra to write, the reason for the change of his hand writing.

I reached home in the evening and told Poornima about the very beautiful hand-writing of Jayachandra more than anything else.

After all I am her husband. She listened to whatever I said patiently and I felt happy. But my happiness didn't last long.

It seems she read in a book, with the help of one's hand-writing the whole of his or her future, present and past can be determined. She found out the address of the adept in the field. She insisted that my hand-writing-her hand-writing and the baby's scribbling too should be sent to him to know the kind of future in store for us. I was in total disagreement with her proposal.

I wanted to make her withdraw the proposal on her own. While I was in such a predicament Murali, our relative arrived as a savior.

After coffee and the other formalities, he told me the purpose of his coming.

A friend of his was admitted in to the hospital. His condition was precarious Murali came to visit his friend at the hospital. He wanted me to take him to the hospital on my scooter.

We reached the hospital. It was the first time that I went there. The main hospital building is at least half-a-kilometer from the main gate. The campus has all kinds of shops including two canteens. There is another canteen inside the hospital. Patients can have all their food and drink requirements there. On a white board in red letters is written "No admission without pass". Both of us are without passes.

Although we don't have personal knowledge in these matters, stories we heard, cinemas we saw, the books and the news - papers we read did come handy for us. We put a ten rupee note in the hands of the guard there and gained admission into the hospital.

We went to the enquiry and told the person there, all details of our patient and learnt that our man was in the critical care unit on such and such a bed number.

We walked in the direction. All are glass doors and every thing is visible to the out side. There are many chairs and benches inside. All seats are filled with people and those who can't find a chair are squatting on the marble floor.

The people attending on Murali's friend came out when they saw Murali. Murali made enquiries about his friend and they answered him.

I came a little away from them and stood observing people who were out side the I.C.U. A T.V. set was arranged there by the hospital management. All people there were watching the TV. Programme; with much interest.

The anxiety, sorrow, pain that ought to have been visible in every face are conspicuous by absence. No worry about the safe return of their near and dear. The T.V. is trying to lighten their minds by turning them from fear and concern. A very interesting daily serial is being relayed. People are very much immersed in the serial. Actually they are there to attend on their dear and near.

After conversing with his friends Murali went in, saw his friend and came out. Both of us started from there.

*****

Jayachandra replied my letter immediately. This time he wrote on a post card.

You wrote much about my hand-writing. That was all in the past. There won't be more happiness than wailing over the past you too sing like that Devadas. But thanks a lot for complimenting my hand-writing of those days, so lavishly.

Feel happy that I am able to write Telugu at least so shabbily. After four or five more years I doubt very much whether I still remember the Telugu alphabet. Please don't be surprised. Once I get into the office and put initials in the attendance register, is the end of my use of the pen. From morning till evening I keep working with the computer. No other work at all.

I don't carry a pen in my pocket. In school days we used to debate about the mightiness of pen and sword. We wrote on the subject in essay writing competitions also.

You writers too, may have to take to computer, totally giving up the out-dated pen and writing. You are sad that my hand-writing turned shabby. I feel sad that I may totally forget my mother-tongue with the technical advancement further.

Yours,

Jayachandra.

I laughed within my self. This laughter is probably for not being bold enough to weep.

Whither is the march of our civilization!

Man is progressing in to machine!

Flower is progressing into bud!

Statue is progressing into stone!

What a progress, Oh! God! Is this life worth living!

****

LIVING TOGETHER

Like a gold flower among tiny grass that blooms: Like the moon among stars' like a damsel in the midst of old men, a very beautiful palace stood in the middle of thatched houses and old tiled houses.

The palace belonged to Mr. Rajasekharam signifying his wealth and pelf. A beautiful garden in front of the palace with a variety of flowers and croton plants in front of the palace added grandeur to each other. The plants are watered with pipes from the overhead water tank. A gardener looks after the plants. The palace, garden and their owner were objects of admiration and adoration to one and all in the locality. The palace has all modern conveniences.

Mr. Rajasekharam was well educated and cultured. He was not addicted to liquor and gambling and was without problems of any sort. The palace has AC rooms. He has two AC cars. At the same time the gentleman was well-known for his miserliness. Mr. Rajasekharam has two sons and a daughter. They were very hale, healthy and hefty having every thing at their beck and call. Hunger and poverty were things alien to them. As a father he was very successful, but as a master he was a failure. People working in his house go round the place and propagate his miserliness.

He won't pay a paisa more than agreed upon. If any body is not satisfied with his payments can seek work else where, but he won't yield.

His work maid Parvathi requested him to raise her wages by rupees ten a month. He bluntly refused. Parvati works at some other houses in the locality. There she begins her work singing the praise of Mr. Rajasekharam.

"Not enough if he has money. He must have a heart also. My man wastes all his earnings on drink. I have to feed him. My new born baby has no milk. I have no money to spend on it. I asked him for an increase in the wage. The rock-hearted man refused mercilessly. He won't lose anything if he pays me a ten more". Parvathi thus got solace – from abusing Rajasekharam's stinginess.

The house wife who listens to her would way. "You people are very obedient to such people only. Surely you deserve that treatment. You don't care for us. You don't have any respect for us. You behave as though you are doing free for us….. you feel great working in his house because he is very rich. All his rebukes are words of appreciation for you. You do any amount of work silently. If I give you a vessel extra to wash you turn arrogant and revolt against me and stop work the next day".

The house wife feels happy taunting Parvathi.

Ramu, the milk man, makes fun of Mr. Rajasekharam and heckles him using all funny words he knows.

"He has such a huge wealth! What would he do with all that! Nothing goes with him in the end. He refuses to give at least a half rupee extra" grumbles the gasman.

Fruit and vegetable vendors, if they demand ten paise more at other houses, the house-wives would say "you show all your intelligence before us. Why don't you ask that Mr. Rajasekharam for a rupee extra? You want to make money from us the poverty stricken! Why do you squeeze our blood – go to him, he has enough for you all….."

"Madam, give if you like or don't give if you don't like. But don't advise us to go to him" they would say smiling wryly.

Mr. Rajasekharam knows how his miserliness is ridiculed. He did not care for all these comments. People dislike his miserliness but they admired all other qualities of Mr. Rajasekharam. He discussed politics, cinemas, rising prices and other subjects with all sorts of people.

***

Suddenly stingy Mr. Rajasekharam turned liberal to the surprise of all.

Whoever goes to him seeking help, is not coming back empty-handed.

Now Parvathi is paid sixty a month, not just twenty of the old. The milk man Ramu gets not four but forty a month. Suppose he gives a big note to get anything from the shop he is not asking for the return of the remaining change. People at his house buy fruits and vegetables without a bargain.

This sudden change in the attitude of Mr. Rajasekharam surprised everybody in the neighborhood.

People began to grumble that his liberality surely would lead him to poverty and penury.

Now Parvathi has no other work than praising Mr. Rajasekharam. "Enough if I can find another such house as sirs. What can the poor folk give me in return for my work?"

Poor people began to hate poor people as worth-nothings.

Workers are very eager to find employment with Rajasekharam. He appointed four in the place of one. Ramu the milk-man is very eager to work for Mr. Rajasekharam. The gas-man is very careful about supplying gas in advance even without order.

Four gardeners in the place of one, three or four house maids to assist Parvathi. The palace became an anthill, busy with a number of people moving about all the time. Fruit and vegetable vendors go to other houses only after selling at Mr. Rajasekharam.

Situation changed in the neighborhood soon.

Work-maids have become scarce. Even those who offer to work are quoting high rates.

Push cart vendors raised the rates of their goods high. Ramu who delivered milk packets has begun demanding twenty five paise a packet. "Mr. Rajasekharam has bought my goods at this cost; we won't sell it to you a paisa less. Buy if you like, no worry even otherwise". People in the locality are troubled by high prices. Those who were happy economically hither to are now finding it hard to make both ends meet.

The situation has become a big head ache to all people in the neighbourhood. People who used to make fun of the miserliness of Mr. Rajasekharam, have now become victims of his liberal spending. Life has become hard for many. They could not find a way out for this problem. Elders in the locality often met to find a solution to the problem. However much they discussed they could not arrive at a solution.

At last they unanimously decided to approach Mr. Rajasekharam and seek his advice.

Mr. Rajasekharam guessed that this would surely come to him for settlement. He was not surprised when he saw the elders coming to him. He welcomed them all with affectionate smiles.

"All the elders in the colony have come jointly! What is the matter?" he asked.

They didn't know how to begin. They sat silent staring at each other. At last one of them made himself bold and broke the silence and said with folded hands very politely. "Sir, Life in the colony has become very costly. We are finding it hard to meet the expenses with our meager incomes".

"What change has fallen on you to make life so dear?" asked Mr. Rajasekharam feeling amused.

"Things were normal till recently. Prices of commodities were normal and were quite within our reach. Suddenly prices rose sky high" he said.

"We are not able to find work maids for our house-hold-work" said another man.

"Even the milk boy who supplies us with milk packets is demanding more. He was taking just ten paise per packet but now he demands twenty five paise" another gentleman wailed.

Every vendor says "Sir has bought this for so much why don't you pay that much"? Said another wise man.

"Who is that 'Sir' they say?" asked Mr. Rajasekharam.

"Who else could that be than yourself sir" said another scratching his head.

"Why all such ado? Quite of late you have started spending money very liberally. Maids want to work in your house vendors want to sell their goods to you. Your liberality is attracting every service and object like a magnet. You are employing workers even if they don't have any work to do. You buy rotten goods at high cost. Nobody is caring for us. None wants to work with us! None wants to sell to us. How can we compete with you in matters of money? You can throw rupees like pebbles. Kindly think of us the middle class fellows. You must help us out of this situation".

Mr. Rajasekharam who was jovial all the time now turned serious.

"My dear friends, I know that such a situation is sure to arise......... True that I have more money than you all. That's why I have AC rooms and AC cars. Truly I live a costly life. That is all limited to myself. It won't affect you in any way. In every other aspect of life, I was very careful. I paid workers what they deserve only. Then you joined the workers and made fun of me and heckled my miserliness. When the workers spoke against me you appreciated and encouraged them.

All those people now call me good. They show all respect for me. I know all that respect is not on account of me but only account of the money I give. Their disrespect then and their respect and adoration now, are one and the same for me.

I thought that you would understand and appreciate me. But you joined them and did the other way round. I know that my carefree spending would hurt you. If I give whatever they want, I know that you will be in difficulty. As your neighbour, I thought that I should not hurt you. I did not like to be burdensome to you.

I wanted to teach you a lesson. So I have changed my attitude money wise. I have started spending money lavishly. That resulted in your difficulty and you came to me seeking a solution. Hope you have understood me" said Mr. Rajasekharam surveying all of them.

People that came to Mr. Rajasekharam bent down their heads in repentance. They felt sorry for their ignorance.

They sat for a while expressing sorrow for their past deeds and stood up to take leave of him.

Mr. Rajasekharam bade them good-bye with a smiling face. The hand he waved at them looked like a hand of assurance.

****

Swathi Weekly 13.11.1987.

MOST WORSHIPFUL PLACE

Suraiah came to the city to visit his friend. It being a working day the friend went to attend his office. Suraiah wanted to go round the city and see places. First he came to a temple.

The whole temple premises are filled with innumerable devotees. Too much of noise – rush – cries – requests – children weeping loud – consoling adults. Everything in Pell-mell. Burning camphor – breaking of coconuts – smell of insence sticks – worshipping – ringing of bells – people coming in – people going out – garlands of beads – vermilion spots on foreheads – smearing of sandal wood paste – chanting of manthras – worship of God with flowers – Vedanta discourses on one side –

Loudspeakers blaring devotional cinema songs – sale of deity pictures-sale of religious books – cinema song books on the other side.

God, standing on the pedestal is watching silently and thoughtfully.

At the very entrance of the temple a notice board welcoming the devotees- states in bold letters -

Leaf worship	One rupee
For chanting the eight names of God	Two rupees
Thousand names of god	Four rupees
For coconut breaking	Quarter rupee
For Camphor burning	Ten paise
For special darsan of God	Ten rupees
Ordinary sacred alms	Twenty paise
Special sacred alms	One rupee

Suraiah was aghast looking at the notice board. He could not move forward. He could not even cross the threshold. Silently he turned back thinking this is not for me.

***

Autos, rickshaws, scooters, cars – all sorts of vehicles parked in pell-mell all round

Men-women-children-old and young running helter – skelter. Fear writ large on faces. Children crying – mothers consoling.

Here too Suraiah saw a notice board.

Admission fee	-	Rs.600/-
tuition Fee	-	Rs.200/-

Special fee   -   Rs.50/-
Building fund   -   Rs.1000/- only.

On admission: for conveyance, uniform, boots, socks and belt – all supplied by the school on payment – Rs.1200/- only.

For admission of a three year child into the school   -
Rs.3000/-.

The principal in his office room was interviewing the parents. Most of them brought recommendation letters from public representatives. A few ministers also gave letters of recommendation. Some are confident of securing a seat – some are doubtful. There was a big crowd in his office.

On one side of the room was the fee collecting counter. The place was full with heaps of currency notes. There was a long queue. People there are gleaming with happiness that they got a seat.

It was like Babel tower.

We are not responsible for the loss of your vehicles – proclaimed a placard hung on a pole. Take a token for the safety of your vehicle.

Cycles   -   50 paise
Scooters   -   Rs.1/-
Cars   -   Rs.2/-

This seems a school thought Suraiah. He was happy that God had not blessed him with children. He moved forward.

***

Suraiah came across a government office wondering at the ways of the educated city people.

Officials were arriving at the office in groups and singles. Each one entered his room and sat in his chair.

Greetings from the colleagues already present in the office – Talk about their family and friends. At last, they settle down to work.

Papers containing requests and settlement of problems. Official note- preparation – of orders – refusals – decisions – whispers in between – pouting of lips – breathing long and short – handshakes –

Tottering benches – leg less chairs – lot of dust – cob-webs – piles of files on tables. Bribe givers and takers – hands between files – currency notes into pockets, Hand-shakes – smiles – irritations – refusals – satires – comments –helplessness – hopelessness – weariness.

Suraiah remembered the definition – "of the people – by the people – for the people". Smile of disgust on his lips.

Party in power – portfolios of ministers – officials – designations – agreements – resignations – applauses – taunts – salutations – show-man-ship - an exhibition.

Plots – crookedness – quarrels – bickerings – accusations – reports – resolutions –fortification of seats – safeguarding positions – attacks – counter attacks – meetings – discussions – resolutions – leaders clamouring for peoples' support in the next elections – never caring for their welfare – multiplication of assets by those in power - wailing of those who missed the chance – Power mongering – differences – slogans – shoutings – long-live – down, down – no security for life of common-man – cane charges – lock-ups – rapes – under all circumstances power-power, money-money-position-position!

All turned round and round in the mind of Suraiah, like people in a giant-wheel. He shut his eyes for a while.

***

Beautiful building shining in the sun. Costly brand-new-car in the portico. Well pruned croton plants on either side of the pathway.

The doctor's name with qualifications glittering in metallic letters appeared. This must be a hospital thought Suraiah.

Nurses in white moving in haste with pads in hands – compounders issuing number slips – Ayahs cleaning the floor with liquid dettol – the odour of hospital – medicines – patients – foul smell - wailings – currency notes flashing – lots of suffering all over – Doctor's consultation fee only a hundred.

Single room rent per day   -Rs.25/-

Double room rent per day   -Rs.40/-

Prescribed medicines sold at the hospital dispensary – can not be bought elsewhere. Unnecessary operations – useless strips of pills – Doctors moving in haste from one ward to another performing operations. Doctors want money – patients want health and life.

***

Money is all important in life. Earn as much as you can – thought Suraiah. Both health and death are sold at the hospital. Even cremation is not free at the graveyard. Many leeches in waiting there. Money to come into the world – money to live in the world – money to leave the world. So thinking Suraiah moved forward. He saw a name board erected in front of an old building.

"Government Central Library".

The place was very calm and peaceful. Only a few people were moving here and there.

No fees to enter the place.

Suraiah walked in to the building. It was a big hall with wide tables in the middle. Many newspapers and magazines were there. Some people were reading them. There were many almirahs full of books. The place was very pleasant – quite unlike at the temple – school – office or hospital. He could have his mental composure. He was terribly sorry that he could not avail the excellent atmosphere reading either papers or books. He was sorry he wasted his time loitering all along the streets.

His village has no library. He made up his mind to build in his village the most worshipful place.

****

Andhra Prabha Weekly 30.03.1988

NOTHING TO FEEL PROUD

It is very long since I have visited Gopal Rao's house. It would be nice to go and see him once. To-day, soon after the Ramayana on the T.V., I decided to start to his house. I completed my bath and had Tiffin much earlier. I sat on the sofa and looked at the wall clock. It is not even nine. Ramayana starts at Nine Thirty. I may as well see Ramayana in Gopal Rao's house. So thinking I put on clothes and went to Gopala Rao's house.

I tapped on the door rather hard, four or five times. The door wasn't opened. There was no response from inside either.

Perhaps they are completely absorbed in watching T.V. or are busy otherwise.

Gopala Rao's son opened the door and ran back. Gopala Rao came out of his room, soon after I stepped into the house.

'Come, come, you remembered us after a very long lapse of time". So saying he invited me in to his house. He cleared the papers and books off the chair and invited me to sit.

"Not that I don't want to come - pressure of work stands in my way of coming to you" answering him I said sitting in the chair. "I think of you quite so often".

"Hello, Brother, how do you do? You have stopped completely coming to our house. Gopal Rao's wife Sujatha came out complaining jovially.

"All are well, sister" I smiled after saying. "But where is your daughter? She is not seen here".

"She sat in that room, annoyed at her mother", said Gopal Rao.

"So, too difficult to speak to her" I said.

For a while we sat talking office affairs, T.V. programmes and of course politics.

In the meanwhile, Sujatha brought coffee for us.

"Suji where are those photos we took recently, get them here", Gopal Rao told his wife.

Soon she heard those words, the baby came running into the room and leaped in to my lap.

Sujatha put the envelope containing photos in to my hand.

As I began to turn the photos one after the other, the baby started speaking sweetly to me.

Whenever I went to Gopal Rao's house the baby used to come to me only after much entreating and cajoling. But she has come now on her own and sitting in my lap speaking so lovingly. I felt very happy and surprised at the same time.

I gave the photo envelope to Gopal Rao and sat talking and listening to the girl.

We three laughed at her words. They narrated the mischief she does and the innocent looks she puts on. I felt very pleasant listening to them. Theirs is a very happy family, I thought.

"So I shall take leave of you" I rose from my seat.

The girl held my legs with her two hands without allowing me to move.

"I shall come again baby" I lifted her into my arms.it/

"Please uncle, sit a little more with us", she pleaded very lovingly.

I shall come again in the evening. I shall bring your aunt and Ashok also with me. Now allow me to leave" I pleaded.

She shook her head in disapproval.

"No, don't be naughty baby- uncle will come again" Gopal Rao took the girl into his hands.

Suddenly the girl began to weep and wail. I took her into my arms consoling.

"Shall we go out and get some Chacolates?" I said to the baby.

She readily agreed.

"No need to go out now brother. She will weep for some time and then keep quiet"

Sujatha tried to take the girl from me.

The girl shook her hands and legs. Her weeping touched the peak.

Thinking that trying to control her will be of no use, I walked on to the road holding the girl's hand.

Gopal Rao put on his shirt and tried to follow us.

"No, Daddy should not come" the baby said angrily.

"Baby doesn't want you. I and baby alone will go. Please stay back" I prevented Gopal Rao from accompanying us.

I took the baby to a shop, bought her a biscuit packet and a few chocolates and gave them to her.

"Uncle you stay with us" said the baby.

"I said to come in the evening".

"No, you must stay from now itself."

"You are my golden doll - you should listen to what ever is said to you by your parents".

"No uncle, if you go, Father and mother shout at each other angrily. I and brother get frightened. "If we weep both father and mother beat us black and blue. When you are with them they remain very jovial. All of us feel happy" the girl revealed the real secret.

When I came to know about the fear in her tender mind, I am all pity for her. Gopal Rao and Sujatha gained only disgust in my mind.

I didn't like to discuss the matter with her parents. I began to think silently.

Soon an idea flashed in my mind. Although it can't be a solution to the problem, I decided to try for the present.

"Mr. Gopal Rao, I shall take the baby with me to my house. We shall bring her with us in the evening when we come" I said.

"Why brother, she won't stay with you. She begins to weep soon you reach home. You have to bring her back in the hot sun" said Sujatha,

"She won't give such trouble. If it becomes so necessary I shall get her. No problem at all". I said to her and started home holding the baby's hand.

"Why have you come so early? You could have visited another friend's house" said my wife harshly at the very sight of me.

"It was a little late at Gopal Rao's house", I said non-plussed a little.

"That's all right. You had had good past-time at your friend's house".

Until then I could not remember the cinema promise I made to her. I offered to take her to the eleven o'clock show but failed to keep it up. That has been cause for her anger.

Her taunting provoked me also. I too shouted loud angrily.

Each of us tried to out do the other. Bitter words found their way in to our altercation.

I thought of getting out of the house though for a little while.

The grim face of the baby who stood in front of me made me hang my head in shame.

"Uncle, take me to our house" baby said trying to hold back her tears.

I don't have words to console her.

Silently I started to Gopal Rao's house holding the baby's hand.

****

Andhra Prabha 21.09.1988

OF SAME FEATHERS

Venkatramaiah got down the rickshaw and offered a two rupee note to the rickshaw– man.

"I don't have change with me sir" said the rickshawallah wiping his sweat.

"What can I do, fellow, I too don't have the change". There was uneasiness in Venkatramaiah's voice.

"There – ask in that beedi bunk sir' the rickshaw wallah said.

"You don't have even a quarter rupee with you?" so saying he walked to the beedi bunk.

"You are my first customer sir" murmured the rickshaw wallah.

The rickshaw wallah asked for two and a half rupees. Venkatramaiah offered a rupee and a half. After some bargain the two agreed at a rupee and seventy five paise.

Venkatramaiah approached the bunk and asked flaunting the two rupee note to the boy in the bunk "Can you give me change for two rupees".

"No. No change with me" the boy answered rather carelessly even without caring to see the man at least.

"All right. Give me a soda".

"Ice soda or the usual one?"

"Give me the ice soda"

Venkatramaiah gave the bunk boy the two rupee note and took the change back.

The rickshaw wallah was right near Venkatramaiah. Venkatramaiah gave him his money and went back to the place where he got down the rickshaw.

It is not clear how many rooms were in the building. But two rooms were quite large. There were more than a half a dozen costly chairs in the first room. There were two sofas. There was also a tea-poy with news papers on it.

On the right side there was a counter displaying a board with ENQUIRY painted on it.

There was a young woman reading a novel or some book. The office was just opened and hence not much rush of people was there.

Venkatramaiah walked in and went towards the enquiry.

"What do you want sir?" asked the young lady sitting there.

Venkatramaiah without saying a word took out a paper from his pocket and gave it to her.

"You have to fill up an application form sir" she said.

"Please you fill it up" he requested.

Half of unemployment problem can be solved if all these women don't crowd for jobs. Why should they crave for jobs when the husband is employed and earning money? They may as well sit in the house and enjoy. Jobs are for men and houses are for women. It is the woman that makes a home.

In some houses both wife and husband are employees while countless degree holders are loitering on the streets for want of jobs. Job is a past – time for several women.

Venkatramaiah was thinking like this when he heard the voice of the lady.

All this while she has been looking at the paper Venkatramaiah has given. "Please give me the information I ask for and I shall complete this form".

"Is the writing so illegible madam" said Venkatramaiah smiling.

She smiled uncomfortably in reply.

"Name?"

"Vasantha"

"Age? -

"Twenty three".

"Education?"

"Intermediate"

"Father's Name?"

"Venkatramaiah"

"Complexion?"

"Fair" "Wheatish"

"Height"?

"5 feet 3 inches.

Venkatramaiah orally told whatever information she asked for. The form was completed and given to Venkatramaiah for his signature.

Holding the paper in his hand Venkatramaiah walked into another room.

Four people were in four chairs sitting. In front of each, on the table was a card proclaiming the occupants' name? Behind each one on the wall were hanging boxes with the following numbers – fifty to hundred, fifteen to fifty, fifteen to one NIL.

Venkatramaiah went to the man with NIL number behind.

He verified the form from top to bottom and put his signature and stamped it below. Venkatramaiah paid the necessary fees. On the top of the form he put a date in red ink and asked him to come back on the date put in red ink.

There was a month's gap between the day he went and the day he was asked to come back. Venkatramaiah walked out though not with complete satisfaction.

He bargained with another rickshawwallah, got into it and reached home.

Venkatramaiah was a retired government employee. He has four children – three girls and a boy. He celebrated the marriage of his eldest daughter with much pomp when the dowry charged by grooms was at the lowest. The second was a son who completed his degree and was working at a private firm. His second daughter was Vijaya. He could perform her marriage also though not with as much pomp when the rates of grooms in the market was somewhat within reach. He had to borrow money to celebrate Vijay's marriage. He was happy that he could send both the elder daughters to their homes. The debt incurred for the marriage was not much and also not above his means. The reason was that he was still in employment and cleared the debt in installments.

Now Venkatramaiah has some property left and was leading his life depending on the pension he got every month. The earnings of his son were of some use too. He was saving some thing for the marriage of his third daughter, Vasantha.

The daughter's marriage was the only problem he has. He was not able to save out of his pension money for the marriage. He went to a marriage bureau to find a solution to his problem.

The number of unemployed youth is on the rise year by year. The number of girls to be married also is on the increase in the same proportion.

Everybody speaks against corruption but all get their things done paying something behind the table.

Parents of girls speak from house tops against the dirty dowry system but get rid of their daughters giving dowries beyond their means.

Suppose some one sits without celebrating the marriage of his daughter due to the dowry system the daughter herself will question "When you are not capable of celebrating my marriage why did you beget me at all? you should know all the consequences before begetting children" that is the reason why parents although they have ideals and ambitions, have to forego due to pressure of circumstances.

Unemployed youth register their names at the employment exchanges hoping to get some employment. Similarly fathers of girl children register their names in the marriage bureaus. These bureaus have the addresses of young men who are to be married, income wise, caste wise, and category wise with their tastes, ambitions and ideals. They supply photographs of grooms to brides and vice versa. The amounts of dowries each groom demands also are specified.

Brides can go direct or through their parents to the bureaus, find the details they want and if it is agreeable they can settle for the marriage.

The Bride or her parents must first fill up an application form. Colours of application forms differ according to the rate. If we go to their office on the fixed day they give some photos and details about some grooms. We can select from among them just three photographs we like. If you want more photos, they give you provided you pay for them.

Venkatramaiah completed the process and reached home. He reported the whole to his wife and daughter patiently. This is one of his good habits. Whenever he goes out on some work he gives an account of the whole of what ever he has done to those waiting eagerly to listen at home.

Vasantha really felt a little discouraged when she heard that they have to wait for a month more. The wife thought that the gap was not much as days pass by so quickly. She was satisfied.

Time passed. Vasantha was dreaming days and nights about her would be.

***

Venkatramaiah entered the bureau office with his daughter Vasantha. There were nearly a hundred people moving and talking. Venkatramaiah went to the person who fixed the date on his application.

The person wrote something on the paper and gave it to Venkatramaiah. He showed a room with open door and asked him to go in.

There was a man at the door. He took the card from Venkatramaiah and sent them both in.

The list of 'Doctor Grooms was in a long bound book.

"Government employees" was another book.

"Engineers", "Private employees" "Lecturers and teachers" "contractors" "Businessmen" so saying a man inside the room gave the books to Vasantha one after the other.

Vasantha recollected how the people in a textile shop show various kinds of saris to customers. They don't speak against any and appreciate every one.

Father and daughter went through all names, photos and details of grooms supplied to them very patiently.

Vasantha selected six photos and put them aside.

"No miss. You can select only three and if you want more you have to pay for them" said the man there smiling.

Venkatramaiah could not go against his daughter's fancy. He paid the extra money, took all photos and said "can we go now?"

"Yes. We send to all the five grooms whose photos your daughter has chosen. Please give copies of your daughter's photos. You can give them now if you have, if you don't give them as early as possible. The one who agrees to your terms and conditions comes to your house to see the girl and you can proceed with further action.
Father and daughter reached home.

Venkatramaiah showed his wife all the photos he brought and told all the details of each to his wife.

"Of all these, whom do you like most?" the mother asked Vasantha.

Vasantha did not reply and went in feeling shy.

***

Of the five Contractor Ramamurthy was the first to come. He liked the girl but the girl and her parents didn't like him.

The second was Siva Prasad working at a private firm. He came with his father and mother. The bride and the groom liked each other. But the groom's sister stood in the way. The bride's parents have to pay Rs.5000/- as gift to the sister and a scooter to her husband. The alliance failed to materialize.

Lecturer Sreekanth did not like Vasantha.

Venkatramaiah was getting more and more worried day by day. The case of the mother was not different. Vasantha was her usual self without worry or disappointment as she has two more to come. She liked Ravi the engineer most. He was coming next week. Vasantha was waiting for his arrival.

In the mean while, Nagaraju working in the municipal office came with his parents to see vasantha. The bride and groom saw each other and the other formalities were gone through.

"If you complete your degree, I can try and get you a job. Will you agree to do a job? Nagaraju asked Vasantha.

"No. No I don't like to do any job" said Vasantha without hesitation. Venkatramaiah was also of the same opinion.

"My son is very much pleased with the looks of your daughter. She has passed Inter and she can pass the degree exams easily. My Son can get a job for her……. If your daughter agrees to this proposal write to us" so saying Nagaraju and his parents took leave of Venkatramaiah's family.

Venkatramaiah went to the bus stand along with them and saw them off.

He returned home and advised his daughter to think well and tell her opinion. If she agreed he would write to them. His daughter's marriage was more important to Venkatramaiah than anything else. He asked Vasantha whether she would change her opinion.

As expected Ravi, the engineer came. Boy and girl fell in love at first sight. Soon they became wife and husband.

Venkatramaiah felt proud and very happy to have Ravi, an engineer, as his son-in-law-that too without any dowry.

Vasantha was very glad that she got the man she wanted to be wife. Her joy was boundless.

All people appreciated Ravi for marrying Vasantha without dowry. The news has become talk of the town.

On the third day Vasantha came to his house, Ravi brought degree text books and gave them to Vasantha.

Not being able to understand his action, she put on a blank look when she took the packet of books form his hands.

"Why do you look like that? They are degree books. You must write first year exams this March" said Ravi.

"I don't feel like reading any more…. You brought these books without asking for my opinion" said Vasantha.

"Very good girl" Why don't you like to read? Soon after your graduation I shall put you into a good job. You have to do a job" so saying he came closer to her.

"Me doing a job!" said Vasantha.

"Why! Don't you like it?" Ravi said.

"Not that I don't like but……… Vasantha hesitated.

"I married you without dowry only because I thought you would do a job after marriage". Ravi said without hiding any thing.

Stupefied Vasantha could not speak for a while.

"So I shall do the job until I earn the dowry amount you want. After that Can I stop doing it?" said Vasantha with an intention to know his mind.

"If you do so, what gain could I get from this marriage?" laughed Ravi.

"All of you are of the same feather" thought Vasantha. She could not escape from doing the job.

Venkatramaiah stood wondering.

Many reasons for women for seeking jobs.

****

Andhra Sachitra Vaara Pathrika 22.07.1983.

ON FORGETFULNESS

That's a petty tea bunk. Coffee, Biscuits now and then Samosas are sold there. Beedis, Cigarettes, Matchboxes are always made available. Two stone slabs arranged in a row serve as seating to the customers. Two persons can sit on the slabs comfortably. More than two cause discomfort. But curiously four to five make it convenient to sit and read the daily newspaper. The rush for the newspaper is such that it turns in to pieces within two hours. If one reads the others look on avariciously for the beautiful pictures of movie stars particularly the feminine ones. The lucky one that gets the paper in to his hands holds it tight as if he has the total rights over it. Some try to grab it from his hands very eager to know about the new film releases and the stars that adorn. Either it is crushed under the feet or thrown into the nearby gutter in the end. A tape recorder blares out filthy cinema songs loud and without interruption. The place near about is full of dirt, flies, mosquitoes and odour of dirt.

Anjaneyulu sat on the stone slab puffing a cigarette and sipping coffee from the use and throw small plastic cup. He was almost unconscious of everything around enjoying the pleasure of smoke and coffee. Suddenly he became alert when a song disturbed his enjoyment. The song ran thus –

"A tiger is not afraid of the sight of another tiger - A goat does not fear the sight of another goat - But I don't know why a man cannot tolerate the sight of another man!" There must be some magic in this. Anjaneyulu became thoughtful. Two men do not agree on any point. One wants to show his upmanship. One cannot tolerate the sight of another. What disease can this be? What is its meaning? It can mean anything. But in the biotic world, this characteristic is limited to humans only.

When Anjaneyulu was in such a fix, a middle-aged man stood near him and said "How do you do sir?

Anjaneyulu shook his head to mean that he is alright with an expressive face as if to question him "who are you?"

"It is unlucky that you can't recognize me". Said the man looking into his face.

Anjaneyulu put on a show of remembrance but he could not recognize the man. However much he tried he could not recollect the occasion and time when he came into contact with this man.

"Come on, I shall give you a clue. At least try with that to recognize me" he said.

The man is not pretending. He is not a fraud. There is no attempt in him to cheat. Surely, he is humble and wants to talk to him and revive his acquaintance with him.

Anjaneyulu was introspecting "who is this man? When did I meet him? Unless he knows me well, he would not have come near and tried to revive his acquaintance". Anjaneyulu began to ruminate.

"My name is Subba Rao" said the man with smile in his face. "Try to recollect".

"Subba Rao……… He knows any number of Subba Raos intimately. But this one doesn't click in his mind.

Sorry sir, don't think otherwise. Please tell me plainly who you are" said Anjaneyulu feeling shy and confused.

"I shall give you another clue. I shall tell you from where I hail. You can very easily recognize me" said Subba Rao with some enthusiasm.

Under different circumstances Anjaneyulu would have felt irritated. But this Subba Rao is amusing. "He is talking as if he knows me for generations and expressing intimacy". Anjaneyulu could not divert his attention from this Subba Rao.

All of a sudden Subba Rao said 'Tirupati' meaning that he belongs to that holy town. Subba Rao laughed a little with hope.

Surely there is a Subba Rao residing at Tirupati and he is related to Anjaneyulu. He was Anjaneyulu's college mate and colleague too. He was transferred to Tirupati recently. He doesn't know any other Subba Rao at Tirupati.

In the meantime a moped rider stopped in front of the bunk and shouted "Hello Subba Rao, Good that I met you……… I shall drop you at your house, I am going that way. Do you have any work here or would you come with me?

"No, No, I don't have any work here. We shall go. You have come to save me a long walk." Then he turned to Anjaneyulu and said

"Well sir, think well the whole to night. I shall come purposely to meet you here tomorrow at the same time. Try to recollect me. If you still fail

I shall tell you who I am……… probably you may relent then"…..
You tell my name and town to your people at home. At least they may recollect me. But come here tomorrow at the same time. I shall be waiting for you. Don't fail to come" Subba Rao rode away with his moped friend without waiting to hear Anjaneyulu's response.

This Subba Rao some how has become a riddle with Anjaneyulu – However much he tried he could not make him out. Anjaneyulu walked home trying to recollect this Subba Rao and Tirupati. He reached home feeling very uneasy. In the meanwhile, he drank another cup of coffee and lit another cigarette.

"Who is this Subba Rao?" His mind was torturing him.

At home his wife greeted him with enticing make up.

"How is it? You look too much worried. What's the matter" enquired Kathyayini, Anjeneyulu's wife.

Anjaneyulu sat in a sofa in his house with head bent.

He wanted to move the matter of Subba Rao with his wife. But he didn't. He wanted to break the mystery himself.

'You look different today' said Kathyayini sitting beside him.

Does she really see a change in his face? or Does she ask this question in a casual manner? Or is it just an attempt to drag out the inside of him? Whatever it is women are experts in fooling men.

"Do you really see change in my face? What change have you seen? Anjaneyulu said.

"Looks you are worried about something" she said.

Anjaneyulu was bowled. He wreathed a story. "You spoke of having our own house and moving in to it. I was just thinking about it" he said.

Kathyayini laughed. "I know you are not telling the truth. Let it be. If it is such a top secret you need not tell me." she said in her own amusing manner.

"Men can not hide secrets. They are not efficient in this aspect" mused Anjaneyulu.

Just then, a Baby living in the next house came in clamoring and put a stop to their conversation.

Kathyayini did not raise the topic again.

That night Anjaneyulu could not sleep well. Next morning he got up late from bed. It was time for office. He finished bath etc and dressed up. Had his Tiffin and coffee. Took his lunch box and started to the office.

At the office he was fully immersed in his work. He had his lunch. Once set to work Anjaneyulu forgets his surroundings.

After the office time he started to his house with his usual bag in his hand.

Suddenly Subba Rao flashed in his mind. He would be there at the tea bunk. Let him be. "I am not able to recollect you. You tell me yourself who you are and how we were connected" he decided as he walked along the road to ask Subba Rao.

Anjaneyulu reached the bunk soon. Subba Rao is there with a smiling face. He went near him and said "I accept my defeat. I can't bear the suspense any longer. You tell me who you are immediately.

As Subba Rao started to speak, the whole picture opened up in Anjaneyulu's mind. He embraced Subba Rao.

"Sorry that I could not make you out. Please excuse me". He requested Subba Rao holding both his hands.

"You come to my house. My wife will feel happy. Have dinner, spend the night with us and go early in the morning" said Anjaneyulu endearingly.

"I am sorry Mr. Anjaneyulu, I can't stay the night with you. My people will be waiting for me. I shall come prepared some day" said Subba Rao.

Both drank coffee talking old times. Anjaneyulu kept requesting Subba Rao to excuse him again and again for not being able to recognize him.

"Such things are common. Don't worry" so saying Subba Rao ran to the bus that stopped.

Anjaneyulu started to walk home in remorse. He was very sorry that he could not recognize such a good man as Subba Rao. He quickened his pace to reach home early and tell his wife about Subba Rao and lighten his mind.

***

Within a few minutes he saw 'that man'. It is six or seven years since Anjaneyulu saw him. The very sight of the man enraged Anjaneyulu..

His face changed colours – anger – intolerance – emotion overpowered Anjaneyulu. His fists clinched, his teeth rattled – his chin shook.

Anjaneyulu had a quarrel with that man in the bus. He and Anjaneyulu exchanged hot words. They abused each other. That fellow caught hold of Anjaneyulu's shirt and was about to beat him. Co passengers in the bus intervened and pacified them.

He saw that fellow now.

That fellow did not turn his eyes on Anjaneyulu but went his way. Anjaneyulu could regain his mental composure only after some time. He walked home mechanically.

***

Kathyayini greeted him at the entrance as usual.

"You look so angry. What is the matter?" she eagerly enquired.

Anjaneyulu was shocked at this question. "A wife must be like this" he said to himself appreciating her ability in mind reading. He sat down coolly and told her all about Subba Rao.

"You ought to have brought him home" she said.

"He had some urgent work and went away. He promised to come next time" Anjaneyulu said.

"You must have brought him home at least by compulsion". Kathyayini felt a little disappointed.

Wife and husband sat speaking for a long while about Subba Rao and how he helped them like a good Samaritan.

Kathyayini went in to get him some refreshment.

"We very easily forget those who helped us and remember easily those who hurt and harm us. Why should there be this disparity in ability to recollect?

"There is some mystery in this".

How nice would it be if somebody unravels this mystery" thought Anjaneyulu?

****

Andhra Prabha weekly May 2003

PUBLIC OPINION

"Starting a convent school these days is not that easy. No use if you don't have the necessary paraphernalia. A lot of competition. Every one wants to – out do the other some how or other" pleaded Dharma Rao.

"Whatever it is education should not become a business commodity" said Gopala Rao vehemently.

"The transformation is complete dear sir. Education is no more sacred. It has become business long back. Certificates have become education and they are sold every where even by the universities .....there is no use one or two clinging to the sanctity of education".

"There is no wrong in what we do. We work conscientiously. We don't like to sell education.... Suppose doctors start practicing with degrees bought, what would be the fate of patients? Papers reported news of law students writing exams with knives in hands, to threaten invigilators who try to prevent copying. They pass exams by foul means and become lawyers and judges. They become trustees of justice. What would be the fate of law and order?" said Gopala Rao.

"Dear friend, you are in the days of old still. Such doctors are treating patients and judges are delivering judgements" said Dharma Rao. "Of what use would it be if you and I alone wail over the degradation of values?"

"I accept what you said is true. Just because many are trecking the wrong path, we too should not take them as example and follow in their foot steps. We know what is good and what is bad. We must practice our beliefs" said Gopala Rao.

"If we two alone are genuine and honest what good can we do to the society? On the other hand we lose all that we have. You cannot swim against the current. We must sail with the majority" argued Dharma Rao.

"We may not be able to do any thing good to people but we keep up our individuality and get satisfaction thinking at least we are what we want to be. My dear friend, nothing is greater than satisfaction and our own individuality. If we sell away our individuality we are no better than dead." said Gopala Rao with conviction.

"I think even those who preach morals also are bribed" laughed Darma Rao". But sir, if you want to start a convent school there must be some special attractions, otherwise all your efforts are sure to fail".

***

"The very sight of children should indicate the school they belong to. Your school children must be different from those of other schools. Your uniform dress, boots, socks, tie with your school name and emblem are a must for their easy identification. Without such attractions all your efforts are sure to go waste". Dharma Rao.

"I don't like to put up such a show. Children who join our school must put on their usual dress. No uniform, boots, socks, ties etc,. We won't provide rickshaws for conveyance".

It will be like any other municipal school" said Dharma Rao in a lighter vein.

"May be it will be worse than that. Whatever your arguments are, my opinion won't change".

"Do you think children will join your school in large numbers?" There was sarcasm in Dharma Rao's words.

"No loss even if a few only join my friend. I am not investing lakhs, expecting large returns. God has given me this ancestral house and a large vacant site. I have retired from service. Surely I have enough to make both ends meet. I am not at all worried about the returns. Certainly this is not going to be a business venture". Gopal Rao spoke out his mind.

"So you want to teach some poor children".

"No, No. The school is for the poor as well as the rich. I shall teach all. Education doesn't discriminate between the poor and rich. It is the same for all. Who am I to draw a line between the poor and rich so far as education is concerned".

Dharma Rao shook his head in disagreement.

"Do you know this Mr. Dharma Rao" said Gopala Rao.

Dharma Rao raised his eyebrows and said "What is it?"

"Do you know why uniform is introduced into schools?"

"Tell me".

"It is to remove the feeling of rich and poor from the minds of children. It was a means to achieve unity and equality among all children. People forgot that noble ideal and began to practice it to achieve selfish ends. Formerly school used to get recognition by the quality of instruction. But now unfortunately buildings, comforts, uniforms boots, ties and other outward show have gained the upper hand over instruction. Only outward show is given importance. Uniforms have lost their significance. Doctors put on white coats, lawyers put on black coats, and police men put on khaki clothes and some others different colours.   Uniforms of doctors and lawyers are not working for saving life or delivering justice. The police are not giving protection and safety to people. Uniform has become symbol of exploitation. Most of them are cheats wrapped in uniform. Uniforms have lost their sanctity and have become symbols of profession. Uniforms have lost their noble ideals.......I don't like to further burden parents with costs of uniform" there is remorse in the tone of Gopala Rao.

Dharma Rao could understand the agony behind the words of Gopala Rao. Still he is not in agreement with his rigid views.

Dharma Rao and Gopala Rao are friends since long. Gopala Rao is elder of the two. Dharma Rao has much respect and honour for his friend's age. If not everyday they met frequently.

Gopala Rao retired as school teacher recently.

Dharma Rao has many business interests. He is very popular with people in the region. He is well off money wise. Gopala Rao sold away his ancient lands and bought land outside the town. He built a small house there and has much vacant site. He did all this on the advice of Dharma Rao. Once it was a solitary house. Later on, a big colony developed there. The colony has all the ordinary conveniences like roads, lights, water etc,. Now the colony is crowded with people and all sorts of houses. Dharma Rao has his business here also and he and his sons have become very popular. The family helped people in small ways. Dharma Rao is very talkative and worldly wise.

All these made him encourage Gopala Rao in starting the convent school.   When he heard the views of Gopala Rao, he felt a little discouraged.   Hoping that time and circumstances would change his friend's out look Dharma Rao helped his friend in starting the school.

School inauguration went off well. Many children joined the school. The rush was such that Gopala Rao had to put up two more cement roofed sheds.

Gopala Rao was very happy that he could impart quality education to his students according to his taste and ideals.

The colony was a little away from the town. Dharma Rao spoke highly of his friend to the parents. That was the reason why those many children joined the school.

After the school is well settled, Dharma Rao encouraged parents to approach Gopala Rao and express their grievances before him.

Suddenly on one day two thirds of the school students attended the school in uniform designed by themselves which was rather costly.

Looking at them Gopala Rao was terribly upset. He could not control his anger. His eyes turned red.

When that was the situation at the school, Dharma Rao stepped in. "Don't be upset my friend. Your students propose to go on strike if you don't introduce uniform in the school" said Dharma Rao calmly.

Gopala Rao has no words to speak.

"Not only this" Dharma Rao continued.

"If you persist with your views, parents are planning to stage hunger strike in front of your house"

"Then I shall close down the school" said Gopala Rao very much irritated.

"No, No my friend, they won't allow you to do that. They want to keep their children here….. They too have their problems. Their friends, relatives, colleagues and others are looking them down because their children don't wear uniform. They feel the shame and want to request you to change your attitude. Please concede to their request". Said Dharma Rao.

****

\-   Andhra Prabha Weekly 04.07.1990

RATE OF INTEREST

In olden days when you call some one by phone "How do you do?" used to be the first enquiry – then used to follow the other enquiries of welfare of the near and dear. With the advent of cell phones the first enquiry has been "Where are you" instead of "How are you?" The enquiries about each other's welfare has become highly irrelevant.

Whenever I meet Dharma Raju, the first question is "Has your bank raised the rate of interest"? Then only he speaks about rising prices, stable rates of interest, insufficient pensions so on and so forth. I don't mean such questioning is wrong but every time he meets me, particularly on all week days tormenting me with the same question is something unnatural and uncommon. Listening to the same question time and again makes me rather impatient and uneasy.

Magazines make readers divine, politicians make the voters divine, and businessmen make the customers divine. All this is to satisfy their own needs. They are all experts in their business. All are machinations to make their needs served. Thinking that one can not succeed in life without patience, I answer his question patiently – and I made it a habit. I think that my job needs sincerity besides businessman – like – attitude.

Dharma Raju is neither a friend nor a relative of mine. – Just an acquaintance – just a customer at the bank where I work. That much is our relationship. Whenever he comes to the bank he enquires about the interest rates and I answer him suitably. That has become a formality.

The proverb that interest is more lovable than the principle is not monitory so far as I know – it relates to son or daughter begetting a grand daughter or grand son. Grand son or daughter is more loving to the grand-parents than their own sons or daughters.

Giving more importance to interest than the principle, many ambitious people have lost their principles and life. They made their lives miserable having lost all their hard earned savings. Cheats offer very high rates of interest, collect deposits and disappear after a short while, with all the money collected. These days the number of cheaters and their victims are ever increasing.

I made a mention of poor Dharma Raju – but there are any number of people like Dharma Raju.

Generally banks pay interest on the savings deposited in the banks by customers. Whichever bank offers high rate of interest customers flock to that. The rate of interests that banks pay to the depositors is more than the rate of interest they collect from borrowers. The time of work at the bank is spent on calculations of deposits, expenditure, profits, losses, principle, interest, installments of repayments etc,. That's all I know about the rate of interest.

But the definition given by my friend Venkata Rao to rate of interest surprised me.

The job Venkata Rao does is quite unlike mine. The very mention of the name of the office where Venkata Rao works makes one shudder. Every one that works at that office is corrupt. I don't know whether Venkata Rao also is corrupt. No need ever arose for me to approach him to get my work done. But because he works in that office, he too has been branded corrupt like the others. Sitting in a bar even if you drink only milk and nothing else you are sure to be branded a drunkard. No body will believe that you drink only milk in the bar.

On a pious occasion my brother-in-law happened to get some work done at Venkata Rao's office. He wanted a paper to satisfy an official need. He had all the related papers with him containing all the details, signatures etc,. The only thing missing is the currency notes that should accompany the paper. He doesn't have the knack or capacity to get the work done. He has all the requisite qualifications sans good luck or the capacity to buy luck.

My brother-in-law knows that Venkata Rao is known to me and so he invited me to mediate and I accepted. Both of us went to Venkata Rao with a little amount of courage, confidence, joy, fear and happiness all knotted in to one. We went near Venkata Rao and acquainted him with our work. Venkata Rao looked into the paper and certified that every thing was in order. "But this does not come under my jurisdiction. Mr. so and so should do it" he said.

"If it is so – hope you will recommend to him....." I could not complete what I wanted to say.

"Shall I tell you a simple truth?" said Venkata Rao.

"I came to you hoping you would help" I said.

"Then you take the paper direct to him. This work can be completed only if I don't come with you" Venkata Rao said. "Hope you can understand me".

"I am not that intelligent Mr. Venkata Rao. To get this work done am I to pay any money? How much could it be" I said.

Venkata Rao didn't expect me to talk like that. He was puzzled a little. Then he steadied himself and said.

"Kindly don't mistake me for telling you this. If you really want to get this done the rate of interest will be much higher".

I could not understand him. "You say rate of interest! What's that?" I said.

Venkata Rao laughed aloud.

My brother-in-law and I looked into each other's face. Both of us were confused.

"Hither to we used to call the money we take for doing a work "bribe". Now the word bribe is out of use in our office. Now we call it rate of interest. It means the money we collect for the interest we put into your work. Each work has a different interest. Each person has his interest. It varies from place to place" he said and looked into our faces simultaneously.

His definition of rate of interest completely out witted me. I could not say anything in reply.

But my brother-in-law was ready to pay for that interest. The concerned person took his interest rate and put interest into the work. The work is complete. "Every interest has its own rate" thought I.

As usual I came to the bank and occupied my seat. Dharma Raju who frequents came to me as usual. Some how he looked strange today. I thought it was my hallucination. Curiously he did not ask me to-day for the rate of interest. It surprised me most. Seems Dharma Raju brought with him a huge amount. He carried a heavy bag in his hand, came inside the counter and sat beside me. "How do you do?" I said mechanically. We put such a question only to those who meet us rarely. But this Dharma Raju meets me every day.

"Putting that question to Dharma Raju is unnatural" I thought. More than any thing his not asking me about the rate of interest surprised me most. I could not suppress my curiosity. It would have bean better if he had put me that question. But without a word Dharma Raju drew out the money from the bag. "Three lakhs deposit for one year in the name of my wife and me. Any one can draw the amount after maturity. You make me sign

those tax papers – take my signature on those papers. If you put my name first, as senior citizen I draw half a percent more interest".   He told me every thing. But curiously he did not ask me for the rate of interest.

I called the attender and asked him to hand over the money to the cashier. I put all Dharma Raju's money in to his hands. Sending the money away, I sat compiling the papers.

"Now that the money is deposited, please come with me to the canteen – we shall have coffee together" said Dharma Raju getting out of the chair.

"Why so far as canteen? We shall get coffee here and have it. You please sit". I said.

"No No I want to speak to you privately" he said.

I could not refuse. Getting curious to know what Dharma Raju wants to say, I accompanied him to the canteen. We sat side by side.

I expected him to ask for the rate of interest at least now. My attempt proved futile. Sitting in a corner I ordered for two cups of coffee.

"Come on, tell me" I said not being able to hold my curiosity.

"You know that my son and daughter-in-law are in America. My son sent me the three lakhs. He had a son three months back. My daughter-in-law is also doing a job. They don't like to send the boy to baby sitters. He wants me and his mother to go to America to take care of the child. He arranged for our visas to and fro flight tickets and every other thing. He offered to care for us well. He wants us to go there" he stopped sipping coffee.

"I advise you to go. You can see America as well as your grandson. Interest is more loving than principle" I said.

"I told him that I don't mean to go to America. I am accustomed to look after my lands, sites, our house, relatives and friends here. I don't like to go that distance to stay alone" I said. "Do you know what he said in reply?" If you look after my son for six months you can go back to India and come here again". He offered to give us each a lakh" by then tears flooded his eyes. His words moved me.: 5 :

"Is it?" I said involuntarily.

"Yes. It is cent percent true. They call this 'rate of interest', he said. That is the rate they pay for the interest we put in to their son". Dharma Raju could not control his sorrow.

I am stupefied. I could not digest the manner in which these words are used.

"Do you know what I told him?"

"What did you say"? I raised my eye brows.

"Not one lakh. You should give each of us at least a lakh and half". I wanted the amount to be sent in advance. How can he escape? He sent it as soon as I asked. That is the three lakhs I have now deposited in your bank". Said Dharma Raju wiping tears from his eyes.

"So you are going to America" I said to lighten the atmosphere.

"Who? Not I. You seem to be very good. I shall make his mother phone up to him this night".

"What would you make her say?"

What will we say? We tell him "we are not ready to go any where under any circumstances. The three lakhs you sent is the cost we collect for begetting you, for educating you, for celebrating your marriage and for sending you to America. Every work has its own rate of interest. Three lakhs is the principle you have to pay us. After getting the principle I shall ask for interest. Interest is more lovable than the principle. I shall calculate the cost of our love and let you know soon". This is what I mean to say said Dharma Raju.

Dharma Raju is really worthy of his name I thought.

****

Navya Weekly Nov.19, 2008

THE NECTAR OF LIFE

"You may say what ever you like but I will marry only him" boldly said Indira.

"Can't you understand what we say?" Narayana Rao said disturbed.

"I speak only after I understand every thing" she answered her father without any hesitation.

"No, No, after knowing every thing we can't agree to this marriage" her mother said harshly.

"Mother, you were exclaiming his handsomeness just three hours earlier. What made you hate him so soon and so much?" asked Indira.

"Handsomeness and other attributes count only when all other things are proper".

"So what?" questioned Indira?

"Words are useless, Indira. We are all your well-wishers… you listen to us. We say all this keeping your future and your children's in mind" Vardhanamma tried to convince her daughter.

"Future is in no-body's hands. All this is meaningless thinking. I made up my mind not in haste or out of foolishness. Give up fear and think whole heartedly. Every thing will go off properly as desired" Indira spoke trying to give courage to her parents.

"She has gone mad. Unless she is cured the marriage will not materialize. First I tell them that we don't want their alliance" shouted Chakrapani rashly.

"Don't speak so harsh in haste" Chakrapani's wife cautioned him.

"I shall speak to Indira. All of you kindly vacate the room" said Sridhar the elder-son-in-law. In obedience to his request all vacated the room.

"I am sorry brother-in-law. I don't like to speak to any one in this regard. My decision won't change" said Indira stead-fastly. Sridhar fell silent and went out.

"Indira seems Satan his overpowered you. That's why you are turning deaf to all our pleadings and entreaties" said Vardhanamma very much perturbed.

"Vardhani, don't shout so loud" Narayana Rao cautioned his wife and silently walked to his room.

We should not pull the string until it is broken. Much more deep thinking should be made in the matter, thought Narayana Rao.

Murali is Indira's younger brother. He thought that every one in the house is speaking quite reasonably. Murali is the youngest in the house.

He has complete confidence in the intelligence and thinking of his elder sister. Without speaking a word himself he just kept listening to the others in the house. There must be some strong reason for Indira's insistence on the alliance.

Indira's love for Murali is boundless. Every one in the house thought only Murali could change Indira's resolve.

***

Indira is twenty three years old. Just twenty days back people came to see Indira. Narayana Rao made elaborate arrangements for the occasion as that was the first time when people came to see Indira seeking marriage alliance. Narayana Rao though not a wealthy lawyer is well known in the neighborhood as a respectable gentleman.

He has two sons and two daughters. The house is busy with friends and relatives visiting them often. Happiness pervades all over. Narayana Rao is not one among many but has individuality of his own. Vardhanamma is his worthy wife.

Srinivas was the groom. His parents and elder sister accompanied him to certify the girl.

Srinivas liked Indira at first sight. Her beauty captivated him. Indira's situation was least different. He was her Greek warrior and he liked the prince at sight. Her mind danced with joy at the very sight of the man. All certified that they were born-for-each-other. Both felt deeply the first sight love.

"If both of you want to speak privately, you can do so" said the middleman who brought the alliance and showed the bride and the groom the adjacent vacant room.

Amidst the laughter of all, Indira and Srinivas walked in to the room.

Truly both sides fully desired for the fructification of the alliance.

Srinivas very openly told Indira the amount of salary he was drawing and the kind of life he wants to lead and the kind of life he lived. He hid nothing and spoke very plainly.

Srinivas' openness pleased Indira most. She too opened her heart to him – spoke of her desires, dreams and every thing without any hiding.

'To be frank you are wealthier than we are. My job is the only property I have. I have told you my economic status also. If only you think you can adjust……..'' said Srinivas.

"My father sent for you only after making all enquiries. But now all those things are not of my concern" Indira said to mean that she wants him only and nothing else.

"Good – I tell you, I have no habits. I don't drink, don't smoke, and don't even chew betel-nut-powder" his plain confession undid her a little. But she felt exceeding happiness. Two reasons for her happiness – One he has no bad habits and two he told about his habits even without being asked for.

Srinivas didn't stop at that. Again and again he questioned Indira about her wishes and dreams time and again. Both came out of the room after opening their hearts to each other.

The bride and groom conveyed their agreement officially within two days. Elders from both sides decided to have fixation of alliance soon and also fix the marriage date.

Indira and Srinivas started conversing through their cell phones. Cells between them rang at least once every hour. The elders felt happy observing them. Before he left Srinivas asked for a photograph of Indira. She sent her photo through Murali. With the consent of all in the house Srinivas sent his photo to Indira. Murali was the carrier on both sides.

Soon Srinivas felt bored. Just in ten days after the first meeting, he came to see Indira. He did not stay long for fear that the others in the house might make fun of him. He came in the morning and got ready to go back in the evening.

Father and daughter accompanied Srinivas to the station to see him off purposely an hour in advance. Her idea was to spend more time with him alone. Narayana Rao sat in a chair on the plat-form and started reading a weekly magazine. The would be wife and husband had endless talk walking all along the plat-form uninterrupted. Luckily the arrival of the train was late by another forty minutes. Much more time for the couple to spend together talking their minds out. Time is not enough for them to talk and talk. To the discomfiture of both the train arrived on the plat-form. Srinivas got into the train but he still had words to speak to Indira. Father and daughter bade him farewell waving their hands. Srinivas too waved his hand so endearingly when the train started.

Indira and Narayana Rao reached home.

***

Srinivas showed the photograph of his would be wife to all his colleagues at the office. Every one appreciated the good luck of Srinivas who is going to have such a beautiful wife as his own. He felt highly elated and treated them all to a party.

Srinivas never knew that the very first sight could be so intoxicating. He kept eagerly expecting a letter from the father-in-laws' naming the fixation date and marriage day.

Then came the bolt from the blue in the shape of a pink slip. Like countless software engineers, Srinivas too became a victim of recession. Srinivas shuddered looking at the paper. He sweated all over. The questions that confronted him were – how to repay the car loan? How to pay the house loan installments every month? his marriage, incoming wife, household expenses – the very thought quivered him. Above all is Indira – how would she respond to the new situation? He was stupefied to think of all these.

Suppose Indira refuses? He could not bear the very thought. Yet he could not hide anything from her. Srinivas conveyed the news to his parents and asked them to convey the same to Indira and her parents.

Immediately he switched off his cell phone. He didn't know what to say and what to do. He switched off the phone so that he won't listen to Indira on phone. Parents of Srinivas informed the sad news to Narayana Rao and his wife.

The cause of all the arguments and discussions in the house of Narayana Rao is this news.

Every one in the house was against the alliance because Srinivas had lost his job and so Indira could never be happy in that house. But inspite of all the adverse situation Indira was intent on her marriage with Srinivas.

Above all, that Srinivas had not phoned up to her for the past four days tormented Indira. He did not even reply her calls. "Insecurity and shame should not drive him to any hasty action" she wished and prayed, hearing that Srinivas had lost his job.

Narayana Rao called Indira to him and said "My dear Child security is very important to life. To live an insecure life is very hard. One must have belly full to eat. Without food nobody can do anything. Every thing in life is after food only. He has to search for a new job. To lose is easier than to gain. For anything it is not good to take decision in haste. We have to rethink over the whole issue".

Indira ruminated over the advice of her father.

"While getting the girls married, we have to take into consideration many factors. They may think that this is inauspicious because he lost the job soon we made the decision. If they speak continuously about your bad luck, we can't bear it dear. Why all this trouble? If not this, we get another". Mother's sentimental advice she remembered.

Suppose he loses his job after marriage what would all these people do? What would they say? Who can imagine? Lakhs of employees are thrown out of their jobs! Each one has his/her own problem. Who is responsible for all this? Among lakhs he happens to be one. Suppose we go in for another, what guarantee is there that every thing will be all right? But taking the situation into consideration – whose job is guaranteed? Whose life is secure? Whose property is secure? Whose position is secure? Who will provide the necessary guarantee? Several thoughts cropped up in her mind. Come what may – I am sure to marry Srinivas. No other thoughts. The decision is final and last, she thought.

Keeping aside his good looks and all that, the way he spoke plainly attracted her very much. Suppose he doesn't inform about the loss of his job and goes through the marriage what can any one do? He is not of such a type. That's why he told the truth boldly. That's the reason why Indira is much more fond of him.

When every one in the house was in a dilemma, Indira's cell rang. The call was from Srinivas. Her joy knew no bounds. She looked into the faces of all that gathered there.

Usually when a call comes from Srinivas, she goes into her room or on to the terrace to speak to him. But this time she purposely did not move from the place and spoke to him in the presence of all.

"You did not phone up for all the four days and now you are asking as to how I was doing. Why did you not speak to me these many days? You didn't respond even to my calls". Emotion filled her throat. Soon she controlled herself.

Until the other day she did not know him and he did not know her. They were strangers to each other. But why so much nearness in so short a time? She is commanding him! God, no body can stop this marriage" thought Vardhanamma.

"Concerning job……..father…….told…….." she interrupted him in the middle.

"Tell me – what if?" she questioned.

"Better we think of the marriage after I get a job, Indira" There was pain in his tone.

"I don't object to it" Indira said.

"But I may not get such a one as I lost. I may not get that much salary. Do you agree to it?" asked Srinivas.

"You may not get a job at all" Indira said taunting purposely.

"That may also be true. Then how?" he said helplessly.

"People are dying after software. Since how long has this software come into existence? Did people not live before the advent of IT? Did they not do jobs? Are the 'software engineers' only people living on earth? What about the rest of the people? Every job is for making food. Enough if you have zeal for work and a desire to live happily with whatever you get by hard work. The world is very wide. Software is not the only job available. If you are not lazy and know your responsibilities, there are any number of jobs waiting for you – any number of ways are open for you.

"Losing the job you have on hand, is really painful. But it is not proper to sit worrying about what you have lost. You can find some job – we can live by doing some work. No work in the world is mean-only we are mean in our thinking. Not being able to honour your own work you honour people doing different works thinking they are doing honourable jobs. They demean themselves and their work. That is due to inferiority complex. Every work has its own social value. All people must do their work. Suppose the sweepers stop work how would be the life of the others. We must do our work in such a way that we bring honour and dignity to it. That's it".

Indira spoke to Srinivas through cell and loud. All people sitting there were listening with interest. None of them saw Srinivas and her parents getting down the auto on the road in front of their house.

"Let me tell you a last word. Please listen. Don't worry if you won't get a job.   Both of us will surely get jobs. Both of us are equally

educated. Suppose we don't get one by bad-luck-we shall start a hotel –
we shall sell idlis and pooris and make our livelihood. I can do embroidery
and that way can earn money. We shall sell fruits and live. How many
families are not living happily selling sugarcane juice? They are all
enjoying the beauty in work and are making their lives beautiful. We shall
be one among

them – we will be one with them – What we have or don't have doesn't
matter. We must have courage and love for life. That's why I am speaking
again and again very courageously. I shall marry only you. I shall contact
you again after an hour. Bye" Indira switched off the phone.

Looking appreciatively at his loving daughter, Narayana Rao came
near her.

"Yes father, several handicapped people, widows, destitutes and
unfortunates are all living in this world, we both are well educated, can't
we live happily? Why should we remain without marriage all our life
timidly?" said Indira emotionally.

"While getting their daughters married it is common that parents
want to see them happy and take all care. But the bride talking so nobly
and courageously is quite uncommon and great. Your marriage should
become an example to the future brides" said Srinivas' father walking in.

Indira looked at them with shyness and politeness intertwined.

The appearance of Srinivas and his parents in the house took all by
surprise.

***

Srinivas and Indira became wife and husband with the consent and
blessings of one and all.

A honey bee knows the taste of the honey from flowers. She
doesn't like any other sweetness.

Indira knows really the kind of man she wants and has owned him
finally.

Together they enjoyed the nectar of life to the fill of their hearts".

****

-        Navya Weekly July 29,2009

WATER DONATION PANDAL

"Durgaiah, see that poles are fixed deep into the ground. The structure must be strong. It should not be shaky and easily blown off in gusts of wind". Vardhanamma spoke these words supervising over the workers.

"Yes madam, we will see that the pandal is very strong" Durgaiah assured her.

Fixing four poles on four sides, joining them with bamboos, spreading coconut leaves on the bamboos, tying the leaves tightly with twine – went off quickly.

Summer was severe. Both young and old are not able to withstand the heat. It is very cool under the newly erected pandal.

Vardhanamma and the workers sat in the shade of the pandal and felt comfortable. They cleaned the ground under the pandal.

Looking at the pandal, built according to her wish and directions, Vardhanamma felt highly elated.

She moved home ward to fulfill the other requirements. Vardhanamma lost her husband in her middle age. She went on pilgrimage to many places of worship. She very actively participated in all activities that took place in the temple. She donated liberally to finance all the worshipful activities at the temple. She was well versed with the two Indian great epics. She reads 'Bhagavad Gita' twice a day.

She memorized the thousand worshipful names of Vishnu and Lalitha. She never takes up any work in the house without reciting those names early in the morning every day. She led a pious life.

She desired since long to start a water donation pandal at the cross roads. She is extremely happy that her desire is fulfilled at last. She spoke to her son and daughter-in-law and convinced them of the need to start one in the name of her husband. Supplying cold water to thirsty people, she thought, was a very pious deed and through that she believed she could attain salvation.

Four very big new earthen pots, six tumblers, two jugs etc., were brought to the pandal and placed on sand so that they won't tumble down.

After all arrangements were made she breathed a sigh of relief. Her face brightened with joy. She was totally satisfied and surveyed the place once more.

She described the whole arrangements made at the water donation pandal to his son and daughter-in-law. The son heard all his mother has said, eating food.

"By-the-by I forgot to tell you" Vardhanamma went near her daughter-in-law.

"From tomorrow don't allow any body to carry water from our tap. We need all water for our donation pandal. In fact water may not be sufficient for us if you allow all to collect water from our tap – all my effort goes waste" she said moving her hands, head and eyes.

The son and daughter-in-law stood listening to her non-plussed.

****

New Jersy Telugu Kala Samithi – Andhra Jyothi Weekly, 07.07.1989

WHAT DO YOU SAY
Mr.JAGANNADHAM?

Countless white ants are born and dead in ant hills. But to what use………….'

Probably the wise man got the idea of white ants just by observing useless fellows like you. It is better to go without children than to have one like you." Jagannadham said shivering in anger.

Satish stood silent, listening to his father.

"The fellow who makes his parents shed tears can never come up in life. That's not good for you. Our agony will never do you any good. Money is not all in all in life, for any man. There are many more important things than money". Jagannadham's face turned red with anger.

Satish stood silent as if he cared least for his father's words.

His silence irritated Jagannadham much more. "Instead of caring for parents lovingly, they throw money at their faces until they die. Leaving us destitute you and your wife enjoy life shamelessly. Don't you feel the shame?" Jagannadham looked straight in to the eyes of Satish, his son.

Lalithamba who has been silent all the while intervened. "What is the use of all this shouting? It's like blowing the conch before the deaf. He should have the sense. He has grown old – but to what use? Does he need some one else to teach him to care for his parents. Beasts are better than these boys". She expected Satish to say something. But he stood like a stone without word or deed.

Feeling despondent Lalithamba continued.

"You don't care to understand the care and concern your parents bestowed to make you this big. No one is born big. But they are made big by their parents with their hard work………'

Jagannadham could not control himself and said interrupting his wife.

"They think they are born big" there was satire in his words.

They are like butchers who don't know love, affection or nearness. Why blame him when our fate has destined us to be like this" Lalithamba spoke philosophy as usual.

Satish looked at his parents one after the other. He said "Tell me how much money you want. I shall give it exactly without a rupee less. You spend it as you like. Enjoy yourself. You may ask for money time and again, I assure that I won't deny".

"Not necessary. If we don't have any other source we will beg and live. We don't need your charity. You need not sympathise with us – Enough if we go out and stretch our hands, we surely get more pity and charity from outsiders than that you offer." said Jagannadham fully over powered with grief.

"It is not money that we want at this age. We want your love, your loving care, concern and togetherness. We want to listen to your loving words; you should give us mental peace and physical health and our final desire is to close our eyes permanently in your embrace". Lalithamba said trying to control her emotion and the swelling tears in her eyes.

"In that case do one thing. Very near the town where I live there is an old age home. I shall admit you there. You can spend time happily. There are many people like you to give company. Every one is provided with a room separately. There is a doctor to examine every day. You have a T.V, and to enable you all to assemble, there is a big hall. There's a good library. You can listen to philosophical discourses and musical rendering of stories from God's life. Now and then I and my children come to see you. You agree to this"? Pleaded Satish.

"You are a moneyed man. You can throw away any amount. People who can't beget children; parents whose children turn them into destitutes only join such homes. I think you are talking with full knowledge of these homes" said Lalithamba peevishly.

"If such is the case I shall put you a question. Please answer "Satish said looking into the faces of his father and mother.

"In the name of jobs you went changing stations leaving me, a tiny tot to the care of my grand mother for some time and to the care of an Ayah for some time. Mother, though there is no need for you to do a job really, you did it for the love of money. Even before I was three, you put me in to a nursery school hostel, and left me to their care. Keeping yourself away from me" Satish was over powered with grief and tears rolled down his cheeks. He spoke rather harshly.

Wife and husband looked at each other stupefied.

"At three I could not even speak: at such a time where is the need for education mother? Did you allow me to taste the love of a mother? Did you allow me to enjoy the happiness of sleeping beside my loving father? You deprived me of these childhood pleasures only for the love of money. Didn't you?........

"Did you feed me cajoling to make me eat more and more lovingly showing the moon and telling stories?

Did you care to enjoy listening to the primitive words I spoke, while learning to speak? I grew up eating what ever was thrown into my plate along with the others, Didn't I.

"Now you are blaming me variously that I am not caring for you in your old age. You are even scolding me. But at that tender age I could not question and blame you. I had to swallow that bitterness not being able to question you. You estimate the value of the sorrow I endured. All my valuable childhood is lost, because of your neglect, inside the prison like hostel. You and your money alone are responsible for that. You did all this just for the love of money. Didn't you?".

"Satish! shouted Jagannadham, utterly out witted".

"Once in a while you used to visit me like relatives. You showered your love on me in the shape of boxes of chocolates and biscuits. You don't know how bitterly I wept soon you left – at least can you imagine how much I craved for the love of mother and father … please think a little".

Lalithamba could not speak a word, but tears streamed out of her eyes, down her cheeks.

Satish's words moved Jagannadham deeply.

"You are blaming, calling me an unworthy son. I tell you mere begetting children is not enough, what reply can you give me? Why do you think about their education and occupation even before children are born?

Without allowing them to enjoy their childhood you are driving them to school with cart-load of books!

"You must make them know the sweetness of love, affection, nearness, belongingness and how they bound people together. They can return them all to their

parents only if they have a taste of them……… If sons and daughters don't love their parents, it is of their own making. You reap what you sow. Why should you blame me for the blunders you have committed?" Satish could not hold himself any longer. He completely broke down.

Lalithamba rushed to him weeping, embraced him and kissed him lavishly.

"What is your answer to the accusations, Mr. Jagannadham? His conscience questioned. Jagannadham wiped his flowing tears with his upper cloth and rushed to Satish.

Satish held his father tight with utmost love and care.

****

- 	Andhra Prabha Weekly 09.10.1996